CLUB TIMES
For Members' Eyes Only

Cute Baby Abandoned on the Ninth Tee!

You heard right, members. While those sinfully handsome bachelors were taking a whack at a golf ball on the ninth tee, they heard a peculiar sound for a Sunday morning on the course—definitely not the kind of feminine squeals these gents are used to. These sounds came from a darling little baby girl with big blue eyes, curly black hair—not even a year old—and a note attached for her daddy. I anticipate your question already: who's the father of this sweet thing? And why did Flynt Carson feel that he needed to take responsibility? Is there something we don't know?

Not that it's any of our business, but does anyone know where member extraordinaire Luke Callaghan is? The Mission Creek social circles are sure missing him, as he's supplied us with tales of sin that made even Mrs. Delarue's ears catch on fire (you know it's true, Nadine).

We like to think Luke is out somewhere globe-trotting and doing what billionaire playboys were born to do.

Meanwhile, Mrs. McKenzie wants to remind us to visit her dress shop, Mission Creek Creations, for the June summer sale. There's a new maternity section for those of you out there who are in the maternal way. And be sure to check out the new citrus-almond oil pedicure treatment at Body Perfect. It's heaven on earth....

Enjoy, and remember, make your best stop of the day right here at the Lone Star Country Club!

About the Author

CHRISTINE RIMMER

"Famed for her deliciously different characters,
Ms. Rimmer keeps the...love sizzling hot."
—*Romantic Times*

A reader favorite whose books consistently appear
on the *USA TODAY* and Waldenbooks bestseller lists,
Christine Rimmer has written nearly forty books for
Silhouette Books. Her stories have been nominated
for numerous Awards, including the Romance Writers
of America's RITA® Award and the *Romantic Times*
Series Storyteller of the Year award.

"Writing *Stroke of Fortune* was such a grand
experience," Christine tells us. "It all starts with
four proud Texans and a baby—on the links at
the Lone Star Country Club. From there, the
story has more twists and turns than a sidewinder.
I loved working with the other authors in the
series, creating the fabulous Lone Star Country
Club, pooling our ideas to make the Texas town
of Mission Creek come alive."

CHRISTINE RIMMER

STROKE OF FORTUNE

Published by Silhouette Books
America's Publisher of Contemporary Romance

Special thanks and acknowledgment are given to Christine Rimmer for her contribution to the LONE STAR COUNTRY CLUB series.

SILHOUETTE BOOKS

ISBN 0-373-61352-0

STROKE OF FORTUNE

Copyright © 2002 by Harlequin Books S.A.

Visit Silhouette at www.eHarlequin.com

Printed in U.S.A.

Welcome to the

*Where Texas society reigns supreme—
and appearances are everything!*

*When a Sunday-morning foursome of eligible bachelors
finds an abandoned baby girl on the ninth tee,
pandemonium breaks loose at Mission Creek's
exclusive country club....*

Flynt Carson: When brooding millionaire
rancher Flynt Carson decides to take on temporary
guardianship of baby Lena, can he right the wrongs
of his anguished past...and mend his broken heart?

Josie Lavender: Being this infant's doting nanny is a
cinch compared to sharing close quarters with her
gruff—and undeniably gorgeous—boss. Flynt Carson
is just the kind of man she has sworn to avoid. But
how can Josie resist the searing passion he awakens
in her innocent soul?

The Carson/Wainwright Feud: For over seven
decades, the bitter feud between the Carson and the
Wainwright clans has ripped through Mission Creek.
Will all-out war break out if a clandestine tryst is
unveiled?

Daisy Parker: The stakes are higher than ever when
she infiltrates the LSCC to bring down the mob. Can
"Daisy" pull this undercover mission off...or will she
lose the greatest gamble of her life?

THE FAMILIES

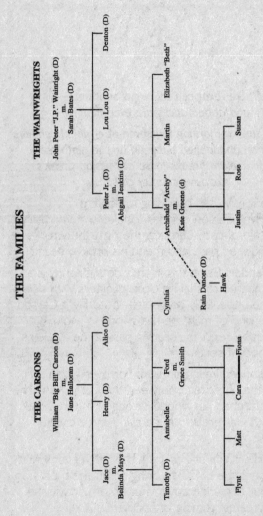

THE CARSONS

William "Big Bill" Carson (D)
m.
Jane Halloran (D)

Jace (D)   Henry (D)   Alice (D)
m.
Belinda Mays (D)

Timothy (D)   Annabelle   Ford   Cynthia
m.
Grace Smith

Flynt   Matt   Cara   Fiona

THE WAINWRIGHTS

John Peter "J.P." Wainright (D)
m.
Sarah Bates (D)

Peter Jr. (D)   Lou Lou (D)   Denton (D)
m.
Abigail Jenkins (D)

Archibald "Archy"   Martin   Elizabeth "Beth"
m.
Kate Greene (d)

Justin   Rose   Susan

Rain Dancer (D)
Hawk

D   Deceased
d   Divorced
m.   Married
------   Affair
———   Twins

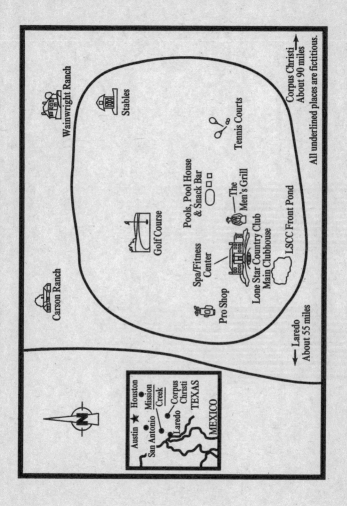

Wainwright Ranch

Stables

Carson Ranch

Golf Course

Pools, Pool House
& Snack Bar

Tennis Courts

Spa/Fitness
Center

The
Men's Grill

Pro Shop

Lone Star Country Club
Main Clubhouse

LSCC Front Pond

← Laredo
About 55 miles

Corpus Christi →
About 90 miles

All underlined places are fictitious.

Austin ★
Houston
Mission
Creek
San Antonio
Corpus
Christi
Laredo
TEXAS
MEXICO

N

For the ones who never give up.

One

The two golf carts reached the ninth tee at a little after eight that Sunday morning in late May. Tyler Murdoch and Spence Harrison rode in the first cart. Flynt Carson and Dr. Michael O'Day, the blind fourth they'd picked up at the clubhouse when Luke Callaghan didn't show, took up the rear.

It was one of those rare perfect mornings, the temperature in the seventies, the sky a big blue bowl, a wispy cloud or two drifting around up there. Somewhere in the trees overhead, a couple of doves cooed at each other.

When the men emerged from under the cover of the oaks, the fairway, still glistening a little from its early-morning watering, was so richly green it hardly seemed real. A deep, true green, Flynt Carson thought. Like Josie's eyes...

Flynt swore under his breath. He'd been vowing for nearly a year that he'd stop thinking about her. Still, her name always found some way to come creeping into his mind.

"What did you say?" Michael O'Day pulled their cart to a stop on the trail right behind Spence and

Tyler. "I think I caught the meaning, but I missed the exact words." He slanted Flynt a knowing grin.

Flynt ordered his mind to get back where it belonged—on his game. "Just shaking my head over that last hole. If I'd come out of the sand a little better, I could have parred it. No doubt about it, my sand wedge needs work."

Michael chuckled. "Hey, at least you—"

And right then, Flynt heard the kind of sound a man *shouldn't* hear on the golf course. He put up a hand, though Michael had already fallen silent.

The two in the front cart must have heard it, too. They were turning to look for the source as it came again: a fussy little cry.

"Over there," Spence said. He pointed toward the thick hedge that partially masked a groundskeeper's shed about thirty yards from them.

A frown etched a crease between Michael's black eyebrows. "Sounds like a—"

Spence was already out of the lead cart. "Damn it, I don't believe it."

Neither did Flynt. He blinked. And he looked again.

But it was still there: a baby carrier, the kind that doubles as a car seat, tucked in close to the hedge. And in the car seat—wrapped in a fluffy pink blanket, waving tiny fists and starting to wail—was a baby.

A baby. A baby *alone*. On the ninth tee of the Lone Star Country Club's Ben Hogan-designed golf course.

"What the hell kind of idiot would leave a baby on the golf course?" Tyler Murdoch asked the question of no one in particular. He took off after Spence. Flynt and Michael fell in right behind.

Midway between the carts and the squalling infant, all four men slowed. The baby cried louder and those tiny fists flailed.

The men—Texans all, tall, narrow-hipped, broad-shouldered and proud—stopped dead, two in front, two right behind, about fifteen feet from the yowling child. Three of those men had served in the Gulf War together. Each of those three had earned the Silver Star for gallantry in action. The fourth, Michael O'Day, was perhaps the finest cardiac surgeon in the Lone Star State. He spent his working life fighting to save lives in the operating room—and most of the time, he won. Flynt's own father, Ford Carson, was a living testament to the skill and steely nerves of Dr. O'Day.

Not a coward in the bunch.

But that howling baby stopped them cold. To the world, they might be heroes, but they were also, all four, single men. And childless. Not a one knew what the hell to do with a crying infant.

So they hung back. And the baby cried louder.

Flynt and Michael moved up on the other two, so that all four of them stood shoulder to shoulder. The men exchanged the kinds of looks bachelors are likely to share when a baby is wailing and there's no female around to take charge and defuse the situation.

"Maybe the mother's nearby," Spence suggested hopefully.

"Where?" demanded Tyler, scowling. "Crouched in the bushes? Hiding in the shed?"

"Hey. It's a thought."

Another several edgy seconds passed, with the poor kid getting more worked up, those little arms pumping wildly, the fat little face crumpled in misery, getting very red.

Then Tyler said, "Spence." He gestured with a tight nod to the left. "I'll go right. We'll circle the shed and rendezvous around the back. Then we'll check out the interior."

"Gotcha." The two started off, Tyler pausing after a few steps to advise over his shoulder, "Better see to that kid."

Flynt resisted the urge to argue, *No way. You deal with the baby. We'll reconnoiter the shed.* But he'd missed his chance and he knew it. He and Michael were stuck with the kid.

Michael looked grim. Flynt was certain his own expression mirrored the doctor's. But what damn choice did they have? Someone had to take care of the baby.

"Let's do it," he said bleakly, already on his way again toward the car seat and its unhappy occupant.

As his shadow fell across the child, the wailing

stopped. The silence, to Flynt, seemed huge. And wonderful, after all that screaming.

The baby blinked up at him. A girl, Flynt guessed—the blanket, after all, *was* pink. Her bright blue eyes seemed to be seeking, straining to see him looming above her. And then she gave up. She shut those eyes and opened that tiny mouth and let out another long, angry wail.

Flynt dropped to a crouch. "Hey, hey. Come on. It's okay. It's all right...."

She might be hungry, or need a diaper change. She definitely needed comforting—and he was going to have to provide it. There was a note, a plain white square of paper scribbled with blue ink, pinned to the blanket. He went for that first.

It was damp. Water had dripped on it from the sprinkler-wet leaves of the hedge. The first part of whatever had been written was smeared beyond recognition.

But it did give him a name. Lena. "Hey, Lena. How are you?" The baby stopped in midwail, hiccupped—and wailed some more.

"Let's see that note," Michael said from right behind him.

Flynt pulled it free of the pin and handed it over. Then, while Lena howled and kicked her legs and waved those tiny fists, he went to work getting her out of the car seat.

The blanket had fallen away enough to reveal the

seat belt apparatus, which didn't look all that complicated: a shoulder harness that veed to a single strap over the tiny torso and hooked to the seat via a button latch between the legs. She went on flailing as he popped the latch and, gently as possible, lifted the strap to free her from the restraint.

He talked to her the whole time, trying to sound soothing, probably not succeeding. "Hey, Lena. We'll get you out of here. It's going to be all right. Hey, now. Hey..."

Damn, she was so tiny. Small as Wild Willie, the runt barn cat he'd been fond of as a kid—and a hell of a lot more defenseless. He slid one hand behind the downy black curls to support her head. He'd done a little studying on the subject of baby care a couple of years ago. That was back before the accident, when Monica was finally pregnant and he'd thought he would be a father, even dared to imagine he might learn to be a decent one, the kind his own father had been. He'd remembered reading that you had to support a baby's head. A baby didn't have much control of it, couldn't hold it up by herself.

Lena quit flailing as he lifted her. She was blinking again, zeroing in on his face. Hadn't he read that, too—that they could only see close up, that they bonded, by sight, with the faces of the adults who held them?

She was *looking* at him. She really was. "Lena..." He breathed the word softly, liking the sound of it.

Then she burped—a big one—and made a funny, scrunched-up face.

Carefully he raised her to his shoulder. She moved against him, getting comfortable. She was so warm and small and soft. She felt good, her tiny body curled into his chest. And she was blessedly quiet. For the moment, anyway.

He stood from his crouch and turned to Michael, who said, "I think you've got a knack with babies, Flynt."

Flynt didn't reply. What was there to say?

The other half of their foursome emerged from the bushes. "Nothing," said Spencer. "If the mother was here, she's not now."

Tyler frowned. "Wasn't there a note on the blanket?"

Michael held it out. "Right here."

Tyler took it and read it aloud. "'I'm your baby girl. My name is Lena...'" He passed the note to Spence. "Well, great. *Whose* baby girl?"

Spence studied the square of paper. "Looks like there was some kind of salutation, somebody's name. But now it's water-smeared to nothing but a blotch."

Tyler shook his head. "So. Great. We've got no idea who left her here—let alone who was supposed to find her."

No one spoke for a moment. At Flynt's shoulder, Lena hiccuped again, then sighed. He felt her tiny chest expand, felt the warm huff of air against his shirt.

Michael broke the silence. "Whoever left her, I'd guess one of her parents was supposed to find her. After all, the note says 'I'm your baby girl.'"

Spence was nodding. "It also reads as if whoever it is doesn't know the baby exists in the first place, doesn't know he or she has a child."

Michael grunted. "That'd be a pretty neat trick for a mother—to have a baby without knowing it."

Spence shrugged. "So more than likely, it was the name of the father on that note."

"The father," Tyler added, "who very likely has no clue that he's a dad."

Michael raised an eyebrow. "You three meet at the clubhouse every Sunday, right? You tee off at six-fifteen and by eight or so you're always right here, at the ninth tee. Luke Callaghan, too."

There was another silence, a heavy one. Flynt hardly noticed it. He had no idea what the other three were thinking. And he didn't care.

His mind had started racing.

Damn. Could it be?

Blue eyes, black hair...

That didn't match up, not with Josie, anyway. Her hair was the color of moonlight and her eyes were that damned unforgettable green.

Flynt's hair was a sandy-brown. His eyes were right: blue, like his mother's and his brother's. But then again, didn't most babies start out with blue eyes?

How old was this little girl? He wasn't much at judging a baby's age, but she *could* be two months or so, couldn't she? That would make the timing right.

With great care, he lowered the baby from his shoulder and cradled her in front of him. She yawned, stuck her fist in her mouth, then pulled it free and seemed to study him, her face a blank, yet somehow infinitely wise.

She looked like…a baby. Small and plump, with a pushed-in nose and a tiny rosebud of a mouth. As for any resemblance—to him, or to Josie Lavender—damned if he could tell.

Still, it *was* possible….

Because he had not been careful that one forbidden night he'd spent with Josie. He'd screwed up royally that night, in more ways than one.

But why? Why the hell would Josie do this? It wasn't like her to choose this crazy, irresponsible way to let him know he was a father. Not like her at all.

Yet, it did add up.

He'd sent her away after that night, and he hadn't seen her since. She'd left town, only returned a few weeks ago—or so he'd heard. Rumor had it her mother was sick again and Josie had come back to care for her.

The rumors had never included anything about a baby, however.

Flynt gently put Lena back on his shoulder. He made eye contact with Tyler—briefly. Then both men looked away. Spence was still staring at the note. Michael was frowning, his dark gaze moving from Spence to Tyler to Flynt and back to Spence again.

Flynt thought they all seemed a little— What? Worried? Sheepish? Could they each, like him, be thinking that, just maybe, the note was meant for him?

No damn way to tell. And whatever might be going through his friends' minds, Flynt knew what *he* had to do.

Somewhere in the trees near the cart path, the doves had started cooing again. A yellow bird hopped across the grass and took flight, vanishing into a big waxy-leaved magnolia at the edge of the fairway.

Flynt laid it out for them. "Listen, I'm taking this baby home to the ranch until I can figure out what the hell is going on here."

The other three men looked at him as if he'd suddenly announced he planned to rob a bank and take a few innocent bystanders hostage.

After a charged moment, Spence asked in a carefully offhand way, "What did you say, there, buddy?"

So he said it again.

Spence looked pained. "Seriously bad idea, with

all kinds of negative legal ramifications.'' Spence was a lawyer; as a matter of fact, he was the local D.A. ''Sorry, man. No way you can just take that baby home with you.''

Flynt curved a protective hand over Lena's tiny, warm back. ''Watch me.''

''Stop,'' Spence said. ''Think.''

''I *am* thinking,'' Flynt told the lawyer. And he was. He was thinking of Josie Lavender. She could end up in big trouble for abandoning her baby like this—if Lena *was* her baby, which would mean she was also *his* baby, which meant he had every right to take her home.

''Come on, Flynt,'' Spence said. ''You know we have to call the police and get someone out here from Child Protective Services ASAP to take custody.''

''No need for any of that. I told you. *I'm* taking custody.''

''And I told *you*—''

''All right,'' Flynt cut in before Spence could get rolling. ''I'll lay it right out for you. I have good reason to believe I'm the one that note was meant for, which means this baby is mine.''

The doves had stopped their cooing. The silence echoed. Each of the men seemed to be looking anywhere but in each other's eyes. A small two-engine plane buzzed by overhead, heading out of the small airstrip at Mission Ridge a few miles away.

Tyler cleared his throat. Michael looked down at

his shoes. Spence glanced up at the plane as it soared by overhead, then looked at Flynt—and then away again.

Flynt grew impatient with all those shifting glances. "You guys have something to say, spit it out."

"Fine," said Tyler. "Question."

"Shoot."

"How old do you think that baby is?"

Michael answered that. "I'd guess eight weeks—give or take a week."

"So we're talking about last summer, right? June or July? Maybe August?"

Michael tipped his head to the side. "Conception, you mean?"

Tyler nodded.

"Yeah. I'd say that's about right."

"Okay, then." Tyler raked his black hair back from his forehead. "I suppose it's possible that she could be mine."

Michael made a low sound in his throat. "Well, guess what? She could be mine, too—though I'm probably the least likely prospect of the four of us. Not a lot of people knew I would be here looking for a pickup game today."

Spence said, "Okay."

"Okay what?" prodded Tyler.

"Okay, you got me. I'm no celibate. Count me in as potential father number four."

"And what about Luke?" Tyler reminded them. "He's here at the ninth tee, too, every Sunday around eight—unless something important comes up. And today, he never called me to tell me he was taking a pass on the game."

"Didn't call me, either," said Spence.

"All right," Flynt admitted. "So he didn't show up and he didn't call."

"Which means the word is *not* out that he wouldn't be here," Tyler said. "And whoever left the baby could very well have assumed that Luke *would* be here. That means he's in the running, too—at this point, anyway. The note could have been meant for him. It could have been intended for any one of us."

"Fine." Flynt cradled Lena with the utmost care. "Great. Gotcha. It might be one of us. It might be Luke. It might be any number of guys. But the fact remains this baby goes home with me."

Spence looked at him for a very long time. Then he blew out a weary breath. "You're not going to budge on this one, are you?"

"You got it."

"Hell…"

"Talk to me."

"All right. Would you agree to a compromise?"

"That depends."

Spence laid it out. "I could pull a few strings. Maybe you could take that baby home with you. But there's no way you'll get out of an interview—make

that interviews. Technically the club's within the city
limits, but the county's been helping out lately, since
the trouble in the Men's Grill.''

Trouble was putting it mildly. A few months back,
a corrupt group of Mission Creek's finest had blown
the club's Men's Grill to smithereens in a failed at-
tempt to kill off the man determined to expose them.
That whole area of the club was now being rebuilt.
And with so many of its former officers in jail, the
Mission Creek P.D. was in something of a state of
disarray. Lately the sheriff often ended up stepping in
to take up the slack.

''What are you saying, Spence? That I'll have to
talk to the sheriff?''

''It's pretty likely. And somebody from the MCPD,
too. And Child Protective Services. T's have got to
be crossed, I's will need dotting.''

''The sheriff,'' Flynt repeated. The Lone Star
County sheriff was a Wainwright—Justin Wainwright, to be specific. Wainwrights were never welcome at Carson Ranch.

''Sorry,'' said Spence. ''The sheriff's office is going to want to know about this.''

''You think I give a damn what the sheriff's office
wants to know?''

''You'd better give a damn. You want them all on
your side if you hope to keep that baby at the ranch
without getting arrested for kidnapping, or something
equally unpleasant.''

Right then, Lena stirred in Flynt's arms. She let out the sweetest, softest little sigh—and suddenly, the prospect of a Wainwright at the ranch didn't seem all that impossible. If it had to be, it had to be. "You'll arrange it?"

Spence shrugged. "I'll do what I can."

"I'm not hanging around to have the MCPD and the sheriff's office and God knows who else crawling all over the club. They'll come to the ranch and talk to me there—all of them, whoever needs to know about this."

"I can probably work that out."

"And we'll keep it under wraps, as much as possible."

"We'll try."

"Do more than try. I want this kept quiet." Flynt couldn't stop thinking of Josie, of keeping the gossip mill from going to work on her. If the story got out... Well, folks didn't look kindly on a woman who dumped her baby and ran. Josie had suffered through some tough times in her young life, but up till now, at least, the citizens of Mission Creek had been on her side. She didn't need the town's scorn dumped on her on top of all the rest of it.

Spence said, "Look, I'm not saying a word except on a need-to-know basis."

"Fine by me," said Tyler. "I can keep my mouth shut."

"No problem," Michael added. "This is strictly between the four of us, as far as I'm concerned."

Flynt looked at each of the other men in turn. "Good. And Lena stays with me until we find out who her mother is."

Spence's mouth twisted ruefully. "There's someone else you'll have to convince on that score."

Flynt understood. "The social worker."

"You got it."

"Okay," Flynt said quietly. The baby in his arms was starting to cry again. He patted her back, trying to soothe her. "Tell me what I have to do."

TWO

The Lone Star Country Club came into being in 1923, founded by Flynt's great-grandfather, Big Bill Carson and Big Bill's ranching buddy, J. P. Wainwright. At that time, both the Carson and Wainwright holdings had grown to the point that their property lines met. It was there, where the two huge ranches came together, that Big Bill and J.P. kicked in a thousand acres each to form a social club.

Four years later, J.P's beloved daughter, Lou Lou, drowned herself when Big Bill's oldest son broke her heart. J.P. came after the boy with his shotgun, but it was Big Bill he ended up shooting, shattering not only both of the man's legs, but also the bond of friendship that had held strong for three decades.

Since then, no Carson had called a Wainwright his friend. The feud between the two families was bitter, rife with dirty tricks on both sides, and as deeply rooted now as the proud oaks that lined the curving driveway up to the soaring facade of the Lone Star Country Club's pink granite clubhouse.

Both ranches remained large—and prosperous. And both families held considerable influence in South

Texas, in the nearby town of Mission Creek, and at the country club their forefathers had created. Down the years, both Carsons and Wainwrights had sat on the club's board of directors, the families tacitly keeping an uneasy peace with each other on the neutral ground of the club.

Flynt himself was currently serving a term as club president. And that Sunday in May, he was glad he'd taken the job. It meant that club employees followed his orders without asking any questions.

As soon as he and Spence had ironed out their compromise, Flynt put Lena in the car seat and managed to hook the thing into the golf cart. Then Michael drove them to the clubhouse.

Flynt had thought at first that he'd head straight for the ranch. But the baby wouldn't stop crying. Maybe she needed food, or a diaper change. Whatever. He decided he'd better find out what was wrong with her before he did anything else. He had the surgeon let him off at a service entrance in back.

Halfway up the back stairs, on his way to the club's business offices on the second floor, he met up with one of the maids. He told her to find Harvey Small, the new club manager he'd hired himself not long before, and to say that Flynt Carson wanted to see him in Harvey's office right away.

"*Si*, Mr. Carson. Right away."

As the maid hurried off to do his bidding, Lena let out a really loud wail. He took a minute to murmur a few soothing words, then he headed up the stairs again.

In Harvey's office, he took Lena out of the seat and raised her to his shoulder. When he rubbed her back a little, she seemed to settle down—for a minute or two. Then the crying started up again. By the time the club manager bustled in, Flynt had spent five minutes pacing the floor, laying on the gentle pats and the soothing words, trying to calm Lena and never really quite succeeding.

Harvey sputtered some at the sight of the baby. Then Flynt questioned him on the subject of baby things—like diapers and wipes, formula and maybe even a diaper bag. Harvey replied that yes, they had those things on hand, just in case a guest might need them.

"Then, go get them. And make it fast. And arrange to have my pickup brought around to the service entrance off the Empire Room. I want it ready there, engine running, in ten minutes. I don't want to go out the front, understand? And I want you and that maid I sent after you to keep your mouths shut about this little girl."

"Well, of course we will, Flynt. You can count on our absolute discretion in this matter and we—"

"Great. Go."

It took Harvey eleven minutes and thirty-four seconds to return with the damn diaper bag. By then Lena was hardly bothering to breathe between angry sobs. The manager's office had a small bar area, complete with granite counter, stainless steel sink and microwave. Flynt sent Harvey over there to deal with getting the bottle ready, while he took on the diapering job. It wasn't the best time he'd ever had, but he managed it. Harvey rose to the occasion, too, figuring out how to fill the plastic bag inside the bottle and warming it up without getting it too hot.

Then there was the feeding to accomplish. Obviously the kid had clear plumbing, because she needed another diaper change right after she ate. After he took care of that, Flynt finally felt it was safe to head for the ranch.

He was reasonably certain no one saw him going down to the service entrance door. As for the driver who brought his vehicle around from the parking lot, he gave the man a twenty and told him to go straight to Harvey. Harvey would make it painfully clear that talking about how Mr. Carson had slipped out the back with a baby would be a bad move for anyone hoping to hold on to his job.

Lena slept the whole way home. Flynt had an extended cab on his pickup, so he'd put her in the back seat, facing the rear as the diagrams on the side of the car seat had indicated. He kept craning his head over his shoulder, to check on her. She looked so damn sweet, her head drooping to the side, those soft black curls shiny as silk against her plump cheek.

He called the ranch on the way. When the house-keeper answered, he asked for his mother, Grace. Luck was with him. She was home.

"Flynt? What is it?"

"Ma, I need your help."

"Has something happened?" He heard the worry in her voice. He hadn't had a drink in over a year, but still, she was his mother and a mother will always worry. "Are you—"

"I'm fine, Ma. Sober as a temperance worker. Would you do me a favor?"

"I don't underst—"

"I'll explain it all as soon as I get there, which should be in about ten minutes."

"Oh, Flynt. Are you sure that you—"

"Ma. Can I count on you?"

A pause, then, "You know you don't really need to ask."

He smiled. "Great. Gotta go."

She was waiting for him on the front porch, a plump, pretty woman in her Sunday best, with chin-length graying blond hair and kind, rather worried blue eyes. She hurried down the wide stone steps and reached the passenger door of his pickup almost be-fore he'd pulled to a stop in the half-moon driveway that curved in front of the house. She didn't say a word as he got out and went to free Lena's carrier from the back seat. He left his pickup right there in front and they went inside, Grace bustling ahead, Flynt following with Lena and all the baby gear.

Flynt had his own wing. They headed straight for it, managing by some minor miracle not to run into any of the household staff or the family on the way. When they reached Flynt's private sitting room, his mother ushered him through. Shutting the door, she turned to him.

She didn't say a word. She didn't have to. He saw what she was thinking in her eyes.

Flynt was thirty-four years old, had been more or less in charge of the business end of the ranch for years now. He also managed the various Carson holdings, which included oil interests, investments in local citrus groves and some lucrative properties on the Gulf Coast. He'd been to war, been married and widowed, fought a battle with the bottle that, at this point anyway, he appeared to be winning. But when Grace Carson gave him the kind of look she gave him right then, he still felt like an ill-behaved ten-year-old boy.

He set Lena, still sound asleep in the car seat, carefully on the Oriental rug at his feet, dropped the diaper bag on the coffee table and tried a crooked smile. "I guess you were all ready to head to church, huh, Ma?"

She went on staring him down for a good twenty seconds. Then, at last, she spoke. "The Lord will have to wait this Sunday. But that's all right. *He* has infinite patience. I don't. What's going on?"

* * *

Flynt told his mother the truth—or at least, most of it. About finding Lena on the golf course, about the water-smeared note pinned to her blanket.

Grace went straight for the heart of the matter. "You believe you could be the father, is that it?"

He confessed, "It's possible, Ma."

"Well, all right. If you're the father, who's the mother?"

He'd expected that question. Still, it didn't make it any easier to answer.

Grace knew Josie Lavender, had been very fond of her. Josie had come to them four years ago, when she was just nineteen, to work as a maid. But she hadn't stayed a maid. Within a year, due to her willingness to apply herself, her good organizational skills and great attitude, she'd become their housekeeper. Grace—along with the rest of the family—had counted on her, grown to like her and respect her. Then, last year, Josie had left them, without notice, seemingly right out of the blue.

Grace still resented her for taking off like that. Flynt had tried to smooth things over, telling his mother it was "family problems" that had forced their formerly dependable housekeeper to vanish from their lives. The vague explanation hadn't satisfied Grace. Flynt hated that his mother thought less of Josie for something that was actually his fault. But he knew if he gave his mother the real facts behind Josie's sudden departure, it would only make things worse.

So he kept quiet—and despised himself for it.

"Flynt, I asked you who that baby's mother is."

"I can't say for certain, not at this point."

"Well, fine. Then who do you *think* that baby's mother is?"

"Ma, I've told you all I can right now. I need you to help me look after this baby, and I need you to keep what I've said quiet. Will you do those things for me?"

Grace looked tired all of a sudden. And old.

"Just give it to me straight, Ma. Will you help me or not?"

"Oh, Flynt. You know very well you don't even need to ask."

Grace took on baby-sitting duties when Detective Hart O'Brien, a friend of Spence's, showed up from the Mission Creek Police Department about an hour later. Hart had already interviewed Spence, and Spence had turned over the water-splotched note. At the ranch, Hart took Flynt's statement and then asked him why he thought the abandoned child should remain in his care.

Flynt admitted he thought Lena might be his.

Detective O'Brien asked the same thing Grace had. "If you think you're the father, then who do you believe is the baby's mother?"

And Flynt set about hedging an answer. "Look, I'll be honest. I'm not certain I'm the father. And I don't want to bring any trouble on an innocent woman. First, I'll need to find out if Lena is mine. If she is, then no harm has been done. She's only gone from one parent to the other. If Lena's not mine...well then, it's no one's business who I spend my time with, now is it?"

It was a lot of fast talk and Flynt could see in Hart's eyes that the detective knew it. But his reply gave Flynt hope. "All right. It's obvious the baby is in good hands here. Spence said he was contacting CPS—Child Protective Services. And the sheriff's office, too."

"Yeah." Flynt regarded the other man warily. "That's the plan."

"Representatives from both agencies should be here soon, then."

"Right."

"So I'll just hang around and see what the social worker has to say about the situation."

A thin, soft-spoken woman from CPS appeared about five minutes later. She handed Flynt a business card. "I'm Eliza Guzman. I'll be baby Lena's caseworker."

"Pleased to meet you."

The social worker examined the baby and got a tour of the main house and grounds. "You would need to fix up a room for the child," she said.

Flynt showed her the bedroom next to his own. Two and a half years ago, that room had been set up as a nursery, with a crib and a changing table, bins of toys, stacks of blankets and diapers, and bright murals on the mint-green walls. After the accident that took both his wife and unborn child, he'd ordered everything hauled down to the basement, where it remained.

Of course, he didn't go into any of that with the social worker. He only said, "Generations of babies have been born in this house. We've got baby stuff, everything Lena could possibly need, stored down in the basement. I'll have this room set up for her immediately."

The social worker wanted to know how Flynt, a rancher and businessman with a full schedule, intended to care for a baby round-the-clock.

"I'll hire a nanny right away. In the meantime, my mother has agreed to take care of Lena whenever I'm unavailable."

The social worker was nodding and smiling. A good sign. "Since there is some doubt whether or not you are the father, would you be willing to take a paternity test?"

"Whatever I have to do."

"All right, then." She produced a card and handed it to him. "Here's the name of the lab in town where they'll take a cheek swab. Can you get over there tomorrow, say, some time after noon? I'll make sure they're ready for you when you arrive."

"After noon. I'll be there."

"Good. The sample will be sent out for evaluation, and we should have the results in ten to twenty business days."

"That's fine."

"You'll have to bring the baby with you, of course, so they can collect a sample from her, too."

"No problem."

Flynt knew she was about to tell him he could keep Lena—at least till the results of the test came through. But before she got the damn words out of her mouth, the house line buzzed.

It was the housekeeper. A deputy from the sheriff's office was waiting for him in the foyer.

A deputy, Flynt thought with some relief. He wouldn't have to bow and scrape to a Wainwright for Lena's sake, after all.

He had the three officials served coffee and sweet rolls in his sitting room and he answered all their questions, except for the one concerning the mother's identity. He promised he'd get to that, after the test proved he was Lena's father. Since he had the social worker and the detective more or less on his side by then, Flynt had little trouble getting the deputy to go along, too.

The three left about an hour after the deputy had arrived. They all had what they needed to write their reports and they were all in agreement that the abandoned female infant called Lena would remain in

Flynt Carson's care, at least until the results of the
paternity test came through.

Flynt walked them out to their vehicles. It was a
little past noon by then. The gorgeous, mild morning
was turning to the usual blistering South Texas afternoon. Flynt stood in the shade of a proud old oak that
had been planted by his great-grandmother, watching
the dust the cars kicked up as they disappeared down
the driveway.

His pickup still waited where he'd left it, a few
yards away. That pickup was not only fully loaded
with all the luxury extras, it was also a V-8. The thing
could move. He wanted to climb in it and roar off
down the drive into town.

He knew where to go looking for Josie. First, he'd
try her mother's house. If she wasn't at Alva's, he
had a pretty good idea where to head next.

The way he'd heard it, once her mother got out of
the hospital, Josie had taken a waitress job at the Mission Creek Café, which served down-home country
fare and had stood for decades near the corner of
Main and Mission Creek Road, in the heart of town.
If Flynt remembered right, the café was open till eight
or nine at night, seven days a week. But it did most
of its business weekdays, for breakfast and lunch. As
a relatively new employee, Josie would probably
draw the less desirable weekend shifts.

He could make it to town in half an hour—less,
given that he'd be burning rubber all the way.

But no.

If he showed up at the café now, looking for her, there would be talk. Even dropping in at that shack of her mother's in broad daylight was too chancy. He was a Carson, after all, a rich man, a power in the community. And she was young and poor and pretty. Only one reason, folks would say, why a man like Flynt Carson would come looking for a girl like Josie Lavender.

A voice in the back of his mind whispered, *What does it matter? Why not go after her right now? When the truth comes out, everyone will know about us anyway....*

He ignored that voice. That voice was just making excuses for him to do what he wanted, not what was best for Josie.

Better to wait till after dark, keep it just between the two of them. He owed her that much.

Hell. He owed her more. A lot more. He'd tried to make it up to her, a little anyway, with that ten thousand dollars he'd pressed into her hand when she'd left. She'd taken it then. But six months later, she'd sent him a cashier's check, paying every penny back. The postmark on the envelope had said it came from Hurst, Texas, up in the Dallas/Fort Worth area.

He'd looked at that postmark and felt just about the way he felt right now—that there was a way to her, that he could find her if he wanted.

And he wanted. As much as—no, *more* than—he wanted to draw his next breath.

But he hadn't. And he wouldn't. Not then, not now. Not until tonight.

He looked at his watch. Barely twelve-thirty. The day stretched before him, endless hours of it, until he could go to her and get the truth out of her.

Flynt muttered a low curse and turned back to the house.

Three

Josie Lavender had the closing shift that night. She hung around to do her cleanup work, marrying ketchups, filling salt and pepper and sugar dispensers, setting up the tables for the morning girls. She left the café at 9:20 and she got home about ten minutes later.

Her mom was lying on the old green sofa in the front room, watching TV. "Hi, sweetie." Alva Lavender lifted the mask that covered her mouth and nose just long enough to get the words out, then slid it back into place and sucked in a difficult breath. Alva suffered from emphysema. She spent a lot of time each day hooked up to the oxygen tank that helped her breathe a little easier.

Josie locked the front door. Mission Creek didn't have all that much street crime, but what little there was tended to take place in her mother's neighborhood. "Mama, did you eat?"

Her mother held the mask in place and nodded.

"Want me to—"

Alva didn't let her finish. She slipped the mask aside again. "Don't worry 'bout me. I'm fine."

"You're sure?"

Alva, behind the mask once again, nodded some more, and then waved her thin hand. She pointed at the television, indicating she wanted to concentrate on her program. It was a *Law and Order* rerun, from when Benjamin Bratt was on the show. Alva had a thing for him.

"Okay, Mama," Josie said softly. "If you're sure you don't need me to fix you something, I'm going to have a nice, long bath."

Alva waved her hand again, but never took her gaze off the television screen.

Josie went through the open arch opposite the front door and into the tiny, square hallway. From there it was two steps to her bedroom.

She flipped on the switch by the door. Her room was just big enough for her bed and her dresser and the small pine desk she'd found at a yard sale while she was still in high school.

Josie's computer sat on that desk. It was a nice one, with a big screen and the newest software and tons of memory. She'd bought it when she was living up in Hurst. Mostly she used it for word processing, keeping her small bank balance in order and for e-mail. It made her feel hopeful, somehow. That she was hooked in to what mattered, and on her way up. She had a car—a not-so-great one, but a car, none-theless—and she had a computer. And she wouldn't always be working the worst shifts at the Mission

Creek Café. She was dealing with the obstacles life had put in her path, step-by-step, one day at a time.

Josie grabbed the hem of the snug black T-shirt with Mission Creek Café written in orange across the front of it. She was just about to yank it off over her head when she heard tapping on the window behind the desk.

She froze, with her arms crossed, still holding the hem of the shirt in each hand.

There it was again. Three sharp raps.

Josie stared at the yellowed blind pulled down over the window and debated. Should she see who was out there? Probably not. Who could it be but someone looking to make trouble? Anyone on the up-and-up would just walk up the front steps and knock on the door.

But then again, why would a troublemaker bother to tap on the window and let her know he was there? With a sigh, Josie smoothed her shirt back down and slid around the end of the bed to lift the side of the blind.

At the sight of the face looming close in the shadows beyond the glass, her pulse went racing and her throat got tight. ''Flynt.'' She mouthed his name, barely able to give voice to the word.

Was she surprised to see him?

Not really.

Had she suspected it just might be him?

Maybe.

Did it hurt to see his face again?

Definitely.

He said, slowly, so she could read the words off those lips of his that had kissed her in places she still blushed to think about, "Open the window, Josie. Now."

She stared at him, unmoving. He stared right back. Finally she held up a hand, signaling for him to wait just a moment. He nodded, his mouth a grim line.

She dropped the shade and went to shut the door and engage the privacy lock, pausing first to listen for the sounds from the living room. She heard the drone of the television and the hum of the window air conditioner. Nothing that might indicate her mother knew she had a visitor.

Which was all to the good. She'd just as soon not have her mama asking her a lot of questions about Flynt Carson. Alva didn't need to know about what had happened between Josie and her former boss. She'd only worry if she knew.

Josie went back to the window and did what Flynt wanted, running up the shade, slipping the latch, shoving up the bottom pane and unhooking the screen. He started to climb through.

She decided when it was almost too late that it was a bad idea to let him into her bedroom. "Just wait," she whispered. "I'll come out there."

He gave her another tight shake of his head. "Someone might see us."

He was probably right. Someone just might. She found herself thinking, So what? But she didn't say it. It would only have been her defiant streak talking, anyway.

She didn't really want her private business all over town, and Flynt was only trying to protect her from the evil tongues of town gossips.

At heart, he was a good man. She knew that. It was just that he'd gotten himself all turned around inside, after what had happened with Monica and their baby.

For one beautiful night eleven months ago, Josie had let herself hope that he might learn to forgive himself and leave the past behind. But in the harsh light of the following day, she'd learned the true power that guilt can have over a man—the kind of power a mere woman could never overcome.

And right now, well, best to look on the bright side. At least his eyes were clear and she couldn't smell liquor on him. "Why are you here, Flynt?"

He looked surprised suddenly. "You don't know?"

"If I did, I wouldn't be asking."

Narrow-eyed, he studied her face some more. Then he shook his head. "Not like this, all right? Not with you in there and me standing out here, whispering over the damn windowsill."

"All right. Where are you parked?"

"Down around the corner."

"Go on back to that fancy pickup of yours. I'll be there. Five minutes."

He glared at her as if he didn't trust her to do what she said she'd do.

"Go on," she whispered. "I said five minutes and I meant what I said." Before he could start barking orders at her again, she hooked the screen, pulled down the window and drew the shade.

"I'm out of bath beads, Mama," Josie called as she went out the front door. It wasn't really a lie— she was out of bath beads and she would stop at the store before she returned to the house. "I'm going to run down to the Stop 'n' Save."

Her mother nodded and waved and went on watching TV.

Josie rushed out into the darkness, wondering what in the world was the matter with her, to be in such an all-fired hurry to get to the man who had broken her heart.

She didn't make him wait.

Flynt had barely climbed back into his pickup when she was knocking on the passenger door. He reached across the seat and opened it for her. She got in and shut the door, trapping them in that small space together.

He looked the other way, out the window over the driver's door. But it didn't help. His mind, his whole being, was centered on her.

He said, "You sent the money back."

"Yes, I did."

"I wanted you to have it."

"I pay my own way. But thank you. I did need it at first. Then, as soon as I could manage it, I paid you back."

"Josie, I—"

She cut him off. "No. No more about the money, please. You know me, deep down. You know I couldn't keep it. It wouldn't have been right."

He wanted to argue with her, that the money wasn't much. That there was no point in her not having it. That she needed it and he didn't.

But he let it go. She wasn't going to take that money, no matter what he said.

Instead he asked, "You did all right, then? Up there in Fort Worth?"

"I did just fine."

Why did he feel so…hungry? A hunger that was more than just wanting to get his hands on her. He wanted to know about her, about what she'd been doing, what she'd been thinking, what she'd seen, what she'd cared about. He wanted to know everything. Everything that happened, every breath she took, for the past eleven months.

"You got an apartment?"

"I took a room, with a family. The price was right, and they were good people. It worked out fine. And I found a job—two jobs, really."

He thought about Lena, wondered where she fit

into all this, how Josie had managed. Two jobs, a room in someone's house, and a baby.

He said carefully, "You wore yourself out, I'll bet."

"No. I'm young and I like to work. You know that. Then, well, you know, my mama needed me so I came back."

God. He could smell her. The sweetness of her. And something else.

Cigarettes. "You take up smoking, Josie?"

She stared straight ahead, her profile so fine and pure in the faint glow of the streetlamp down the block. She looked as sweet as an angel—an angry angel, right then. "I don't much like your tone, you know that, Flynt?"

He put his hands on the steering wheel and held on tight to keep from reaching for her. "It was a simple question. You can just answer yes or no."

"I just got off work and I work at the café." She shot him a charged look, then faced front again. "The Mission Creek Café—which I'm sure you already know."

He understood what she was telling him. At the Mission Creek Café, there were ashtrays on the tables and smokers lit up whenever they felt the urge.

"Not that it's any of your business," she said.

"I'd hate to see you do that to yourself, that's all," he told her softly.

She sent him another glance. "Well, don't worry.

I'm not. And if I ever considered takin' up the habit, all I have to do is look at my poor mama to change my mind right quick."

Flynt was pleased to hear her say that. He wanted the best for her. And that included good health—both for herself and for Lena. He didn't want to think that she'd been smoking around Lena or, worse, before Lena was born.

But she said she hadn't and he decided to believe her. "Well," he said. "Good."

She didn't say anything, just went on staring out the windshield.

He scoured his mind for a way to get around grace-fully to the subject of Lena. But there was no graceful way to ask a woman if, just possibly, she'd borne his child and then left her on the golf course at the Lone Star Country Club.

So he fell back on a safer subject. "How is your mom doing, anyway?"

She sent him another iceberg of a look. "What is this, Flynt? You came knockin' on my bedroom window at ten o'clock at night to ask me how I liked it up in Hurst and find out how my mama's doing?"

"Josie, I..."

"You what?"

Did you have my baby? Is Lena ours?

The questions were there; he just couldn't quite bring himself to ask them. Yet.

She waited. When he gave her only silence, she

started in on him again, her voice dripping with sarcasm. "Well, let's see. I already told you about my life in Hurst. So, about my mama... Well, Flynt, my mama is sick. She will never be well again. But she is better than she was three weeks ago. The doctor says she's improved enough to live on her own now, for a while. I'll be getting my own place soon. But if you really came here tonight to tell me you want me out of town, you're flat out of luck. My mama needs someone nearby that she can count on. Since my father's no longer among the living and I'm their only child, no one else fits that description but me." She left off and just glared at him for a minute, those eyes of hers daring him to speak. He didn't.

She let out a hard huff of air. "So then, satisfied? Did you find out what you wanted to know? I don't want your ten thousand dollars and my mama is not well. And if that's all, I'm getting out of here." She leaned on the latch and the door opened a crack.

He reached across her, grabbed the armrest and yanked it shut, his arm brushing her breasts in the process.

Both of them gasped. He jerked his arm back to his own side of the cab.

There was a silence—one with way too much heat in it. He stared at her profile some more, and then his gaze traveled downward.

Too bad he couldn't see much in the shadows. He

didn't think she looked heavier or much different at all from the way he remembered her.

And damn. It was nothing short of bizarre to sit here, less than three feet from her, and wonder if she had borne his child.

He couldn't tell. Shouldn't there be something, some clue? Wouldn't she have put on weight, the way Monica did?

He frowned. Not necessarily. Not all women were like Monica. Josie could be the kind who breezed through a pregnancy, hardly showing a sign, back to her former weight shortly after delivery.

She turned to him at last, her pale, thick hair catching the light, glimmering like moonbeams. He thought about burying his face in it, about the warmth of it, the warmth of her.

"Well?" she demanded.

"Josie, we've got to talk."

She gave him another long, angry stare. "Well, all right. Why don't you say it, then? Whatever it is."

He studied her face, unsure. Her behavior and everything she'd said so far indicated that she had no clue why he'd sought her out.

But did those eyes say otherwise?

He just couldn't say with any certainty.

And he still didn't know where the hell to begin.

She let out a small, hard sound of impatience. "Flynt. I am not gonna sit here all night waiting for you to figure out what you want to say to me."

There was probably no good place to start, so he gave up on trying to do it gracefully. He just told her, said what had happened that day, from the foursome on the ninth tee all the way to how Lena was now safe at the ranch.

By the time he finished, he was the one staring out the windshield. He didn't have to turn to know she was watching him.

He made himself face her. "Look, Lena's safe now, that's what matters. And whatever—*however*—this happened, it can all be worked out. No one has to be to blame. Do you understand?"

She only looked at him.

He said, slowly and carefully, "I want you to tell me the truth. Is Lena ours?"

Her eyes were huge and dark as she slowly shook her head.

No.

By God, she was telling him no, that Lena wasn't hers…wasn't his. Wasn't *theirs*…

She might as well have poleaxed him, popped him right between the eyes with a steel pipe.

He'd expected her to admit it.

But she hadn't.

And now that she'd denied it, did he believe her?

He wasn't sure. Josie Lavender was an honest woman, he knew that in his heart. And yet…

She was so young. Maybe the prospect of taking care of Lena alone had been too much for her. Maybe she'd made the desperate mistake of leaving their baby for him to find and now she didn't know how to admit what she'd done.

Those huge eyes had gone soft and deep. "Oh, Flynt." She barely mouthed the words. "I'm so sorry…"

What the hell did she mean by that?

He couldn't stop himself. He leaned across the seat and grabbed her. "Tell me, Josie." He gave her a hard shake. "Tell me the truth."

"Let go of me," she commanded in a low voice. "I mean it, Flynt. Let me go now."

He looked down at his own hands, at his fingers digging into the smooth skin of her arms. And he hated himself.

"God." He released her, retreating to his own side of the cab. "I'm sorry." He fisted a hand, hit the steering wheel with it. "It's just… It's no good, Josie. You can't hide the truth from me forever. I'm going to find out."

"I gave you the truth." She met his gaze dead-on. "I didn't get pregnant from that night we spent together. I didn't have your baby. I didn't have any baby. Ever. I don't know where that baby came from, but she is not mine."

He felt compelled to warn her what would happen next. "I'm taking a test tomorrow. We'll know in two weeks or so if that baby is mine. If she's mine, then she's yours. There's been no one else but you. Do you understand? The truth will come out, one way or the other.''

She was leaning on the door again. "I have to go."

"Josie—"

"Just leave me alone, Flynt Carson. Just stay out of my life." She pushed the door wide and jumped to the ground. Then she headed off down the street, walking fast, not looking back.

It took all the willpower he had in him, but he didn't go after her.

Four

Flynt should have gone home and he knew it.

But he couldn't face the questions in his mother's eyes right then—let alone the ones his father kept asking outright.

Ford Carson had come in from checking some downed fences with Flynt's younger brother, Matt, around four that afternoon. He'd gone looking for his wife and found her tending a baby.

He'd had a lot of questions, and he'd wanted answers on the spot. Ford was a fair and reasonable man, but he liked things clear and he liked them in order. Either Flynt had a daughter or he didn't. And if he did, who was the mother—and why the hell wasn't she taking care of her baby the way a mother should?

Flynt refused to give the old man the answers he demanded. So things were a little tense in the Carson house right then. Flynt wouldn't put it past his dad to come after him again that night. Ford would get nowhere, but that wouldn't stop him from trying.

After the grim and unsatisfying confrontation with Josie, Flynt just didn't feel up to fielding more questions from his father. So when he came to the turnoff that led to the club, he took it. He found himself a nice, dim corner in the temporary structure they'd set up to house the bombed-out Men's Grill until the big-time architect they'd hired could finish building them a new one.

A young waitress, one he'd seen a lot around the club, Ginger Walton, came trotting up to take his order. "Your usual, right?"

He nodded.

"Then I can serve it to you." It took him a moment to catch her meaning. She must be under twenty-one, which meant she'd be required to let the other wait-resses handle the liquor orders when she worked in the Men's Grill.

But Flynt presented no problem for her. His "usual," for the last year and a half, anyway, was club soda on ice.

When she returned with his drink, she had another waitress with her, a dark-eyed, faintly exotic-looking blonde. Flynt suppressed a sigh. There were a few drawbacks to the job of club president. One was the way the staff seemed to think he was just dying to meet each and every one of them. He never had the heart to disillusion them, so he was always saying hi and shaking hands. He did his best to keep their names straight, but there were a lot of them. Luckily for him, the majority wore name tags.

"Mr. Carson, this is Daisy Parker," Ginger said.

"She's new. We've trained her in the Yellow Rose."
The Yellow Rose Café was the more casual of the
other two restaurants at the club. "Now I'm showing
her around the Men's Grill." At the club, the wait
staff received training in all three of the club's restaurants. That way they could work wherever Harvey
needed them.

"Daisy." He frowned. Something about her was
familiar, he just couldn't put his finger on what—then
again, maybe not. He shrugged. "Nice to meet you.
Welcome to the Lone Star Country Club."

Daisy Parker made a few polite noises. Then Ginger set his club soda in front of him and the two
waitresses left him in peace. Flynt sipped his gutless
drink and wished it was a Chivas on the rocks and
stared into the middle distance, thinking of Josie,
wondering if she might have been telling the truth
when she said that Lena wasn't theirs.

No. More likely, she was lying in bed in that run-
down shack of her mother's right about now, crying
herself to sleep, eaten up by guilt over what she had
done.

Ginger and the new waitress had retreated to one
of the staff stations and begun folding the white linen
napkins, each monogrammed with the letters *LSCC*,
that were used in the Men's Grill and in the Empire
Room, the club's most expensive restaurant.

The blonde said something, and Ginger laughed
softly, not loud enough to disturb any of the men

smoking their cigars and sipping their whiskeys nearby. Then she leaned close to Daisy and whispered something in her ear. Daisy nodded, murmured a low reply. Flynt wondered again if he'd met the blonde somewhere before.

"Flynt," said a voice at his shoulder. "How are you?" It was Judge Carl Bridges, stern-faced and sad-eyed as ever.

"Carl." The men shook hands.

The judge indicated the empty chair opposite Flynt. "Mind if I join you?"

Flynt did mind. He'd rather sit and brood over Josie Lavender and the baby that might or might not be his. But his mama didn't bring him up to be outright rude. Besides, he owed the white-haired judge for getting him and his war-hero buddies out of a major jam in the past, owed him big time. If Carl Bridges didn't want to drink alone, Flynt would provide the company he needed. Anytime. Anywhere. "Be my guest."

Carl took the chair and signaled for a waitress. Ginger sent over the new blonde, who greeted him politely and took his order of a bourbon and water on ice.

"Well," Carl said when the waitress left them. "Heard from Luke Callaghan lately? I've been trying to get a hold of him, but he's not picking up the phone at the estate and his staff there is downright evasive about where the hell he could be." Luke had more

money than the Carsons and the Wainwrights com-
bined. He owned a huge place out at nearby Lake
Maria that everyone referred to as "the estate." Carl
chuckled. "I suppose he's halfway around the world
right now, playing baccarat at Monte Carlo, with a
gorgeous woman hanging on his arm."

Flynt shrugged. He'd always known there was
more to Luke than the playboy image he showed to
the world. They'd gone to the Virginia Military Institute together, served in the Gulf conflict side by
side and even helped their former commander ferret
out a money-laundering ring run out of the MCPD a
few months back—the ring responsible for the bomb-
ing of the Men's Grill, as a matter of fact. There was
no better man to have at your back in a tough situation.

But he didn't know where Luke was, and he told
the judge as much. "All I know is he didn't make the
golf game this morning. If he's in town, Luke always
makes the game."

Daisy returned with Carl's drink. He gave her a
warm smile and a wink and then waited until she went
back to folding napkins before he leaned across the
table and pitched his voice low. "I heard your game
this morning was interrupted at the ninth tee."

Flynt suppressed a groan. "Who told you that?"

"What can I say? I have my sources, both at the
MCPD and in the sheriff's office."

Hell. He'd known this would happen. Once Spence

Harrison dragged the police and social services into the situation, all hope of keeping the story quiet was gone. "I'm trying to keep it low-key, Carl."

"I understand. The child is at the ranch, right? Grace is looking after her?"

"Is there anything you *don't* know?"

Carl chuckled again. "Very little, and that's a fact."

What could he say? "Your sources have it right."

"You're keeping her?"

"If you mean, will she be staying at the ranch for a while, then yes. She will. Tomorrow we'll start the search for a nanny."

"And then what?"

"Damn it, Carl. You can be as nosy as a maiden aunt."

Carl raised his glass to Flynt in a quick salute. "You know how I am." He took a sip. "I like to keep on top of what's happening in my district."

"Yeah, well." Flynt picked up his club soda and drank the rest of it. He set the glass down. "To put it to you straight, I don't really know what's happening. I'm taking a paternity test tomorrow. We'll have to wait for the results."

"Ah," said the judge. "Of course. I see…"

By Tuesday morning, the story of the mystery baby abandoned on the golf course for three war heroes and a top heart surgeon to find was all over town. All the waitresses at the Mission Creek Café were talking about it.

Josie had the early shift that day. When she went in the back room for her midmorning break, another waitress, Margie Dodd, signaled her over and showed her the ad in the *Mission Creek Clarion.*

"See there." Margie sucked on a cigarette and blew out a stream of smoke through her nose, tapping a finger at the place she wanted Josie to see. "They're lookin' for a nanny out at Carson Ranch. Gotta be for the mystery baby."

Josie knew she ought to just shake her head, shrug, mutter something meaningless and step outside for her break. But she did no such thing. She set down the Coke she'd poured for herself and she looked at the paper spread out on the table, at the words in bold print right where Margie's long red fingernail was pointing. "Loving, experienced nanny sought. Live-in position. Excellent salary, full benefits. References required. Inquire at Carson Ranch."

Josie stared at that ad and couldn't stop a certain image from flashing through her mind—the image of Flynt's face, as he'd looked the other night. So bleak. So lonely. Staring at her through the darkness, demanding that she admit the abandoned baby was theirs.

Her throat closed up, just the way it had when she first raised the blind and saw him there beyond the glass. Oh, she was a sucker for Flynt Carson, and that was a plain fact.

He was exactly the kind of man she'd sworn she'd never let herself get near—tortured and troubled, with an alcohol problem. Truly, considering the daddy she'd had, and the things that had happened in her life so far, she ought to know better.

She *did* know better.

But sometimes a person's heart just loved where it wanted to, no matter that her brain kept ordering it to stop.

Margie let out a dry cackle of laughter. "The mystery baby is Flynt Carson's, did you hear that?"

Josie swallowed. Hard. "I heard it, but—"

"No buts about it. It's his baby and he ain't sayin' who the mother is."

"Maybe he doesn't know."

Margie blew out more smoke and squinted at Josie through the thick fringe of her false eyelashes. "Yeah. Right. Now *that* makes a lot of sense."

"Maybe he's not even the father. The way I heard the story, they're not sure who the father is."

Margie grunted. "Oh, come on. Flynt Carson knows that's his baby. I'll bet a month's worth of tips on it. If he didn't know for sure, that baby wouldn't be out at Carson Ranch right now. We wouldn't be standin' here readin' this ad for a lovin' and experienced nanny—and he's gotta know who the mama is, too. He's protecting her, that's all. She'll be ass-deep in alligators when the truth finally comes out. And she should be, too, walkin' off and leavin' her kid like she did.''

''Margie, we have no right to go judging a woman when we didn't see how it happened, and we don't know why she did what she did. Come to think of it, we don't even know for sure it was the baby's mama that left her.''

''It was the baby's mama. Everyone says so.''

''Well, maybe everyone is wrong. Maybe it was someone else altogether who left that baby on the golf course.''

''Humph,'' Margie said and dragged hard on her cigarette. ''Someone else like who?''

''Well, now, how would I know?''

Margie tipped her red head back and blew a couple of perfect smoke rings. ''You said it. You *don't* know. It was the mother that did it. Mark my words.''

''Wow.'' Ellie Switzer, who was eighteen and very sweet and constantly getting her orders mixed up, craned over Josie's shoulder to look at the ad. Ellie let out a dreamy sigh. ''The Carson Ranch. I'd like to look around that place. They say the house is gigantic, got a pool and gorgeous gardens. And those twins. What a life, huh?'' Besides a younger brother, Flynt had twin sisters, Fiona and Cara; the twins were in their twenties. ''I wouldn't mind being them.''

''Well, you ain't,'' said Margie with another dry cackle. She puffed on her coffin nail some more.

"And if you got questions about the Carson place, ask Josie here. She used to work for 'em. She was their housekeeper.'' Josie must have flinched, because Margie did some more cackling. "Didn't think I knew that, did you? I got my ear to the ground, girl, and don't you forget it.''

Josie shrugged. This was Mission Creek, she reminded herself. And people did talk. "It's no secret that I worked for them," she said with an offhand shrug.

Ellie giggled in delight. "You did, Josie, really? As their housekeeper?''

"That's right.''

"Oh, tell me. What's Fiona like? And that Flynt— he is one fine-lookin' man.''

"Humph," said Margie. "Fine-lookin', he may be. But you heard about what happened to his wife, didn't you? And that other baby—the one his wife was carryin' the night she died?''

"I read all about it, right there in the *Clarion*," Ellie declared. "They said it wasn't his fault. The road was icy, and he spun out.''

"Humph.''

"It wasn't his fault," Ellie insisted. "And you have to admit—'' she made a motion of fanning herself "—he is so hot. And Matt, too. They're both just to-die-for handsome, rich as they come and sort of…dangerous, you know?''

Josie wondered why she was still standing here,

listening to this. She picked up her Coke and started to turn away. But the stars in Ellie's eyes stopped her. Everybody had dreams, everybody longed for things they'd probably never get. It was human nature to fantasize a little about the folks who seemed to have it all.

"Come on, Josie," Ellie pleaded. "Tell me. What's that Fiona Carson like?"

Josie surprised herself by answering frankly, "Spoiled and kind of spiteful sometimes. Way too wild. And a better person deep down than she even knows."

"And Cara?"

"Just as beautiful as her sister."

"Well, I know that. They are identical, after all."

Josie grinned. "You didn't let me finish. I wanted to say she's just as beautiful as Fiona, but in a softer, gentler way."

"What about Matt?"

"Matt Carson is—"

Just then their boss, Gus Andros, came striding in from the main part of the restaurant, grousing as he came. "You think I pay you to hang around back here and yack? Margie, your break's over. Ellie, your break ain't started yet. The both of you, get out on the floor."

The two waitresses bustled off, Margie grumbling, Ellie looking worried. The younger waitress still hadn't caught on that Gus's bark beat his bite by a country mile.

Gus sent Josie a glare. "You got six minutes left."

Josie gave him her sweetest smile. "You bet."

He followed the other two waitresses out. Josie sipped from her Coke and sank to the ladderback chair Margie had vacated. The paper was still open on the Formica-topped table. Josie read the ad again.

And thought of Flynt.

Of the stricken look in his eyes when she told him that the baby he'd found wasn't hers.

Oh, he had wanted that. Wanted it bad, for the baby named Lena to be theirs.

Loving, experienced nanny sought. Live-in position...

Josie set down her Coke and stared into the distance, thinking things she knew very well she shouldn't be letting herself think.

Things like how it was high time Flynt Carson got over what had happened in the past and learned to love again. Things like how he so clearly *wanted* to do that. That look in his eyes the other night had said it all. He was just about desperate for another chance—a chance to do things right, to know true love. To have a family of his own at last.

He was a rich man, but fortune had never smiled on him. Not in the most important sense. He didn't have the things that really mattered. He didn't—

"Stop," Josie whispered under her breath. "No. Don't go there."

She slapped that paper shut, so she couldn't see the ad. Then she grabbed her Coke and she took a long sip, thinking that once again she was listening to her silly heart when she ought to be using her head.

The Coke had left a wet ring on the battered surface of the table. She rubbed it away, scrubbing hard with the heel of her hand at first, then more gently. And then, idly, tracing the crude shape of a heart that someone had scratched there Lord knew how long ago.

It's been almost a year, a soft voice whispered in the back of her mind as her finger followed the rough outline of that heart.

Almost a year—and she hadn't gotten over that man yet.

From the way he'd looked at her Sunday night, *he* hadn't gotten over *her,* either.

They did have something, together, the two of them. Something powerful. Something true.

Maybe that lost little baby he'd found on the golf course could show them the way to each other.

Maybe it was high time that good fortune—real, true good fortune, which Josie knew very well was a matter of the heart—finally smiled on them both.

Maybe, she thought, she should help that good fortune along by taking a drive out to Carson Ranch.

Five

The new housekeeper's name was Anita. She led Josie to a small room off the kitchen and took her single letter of reference.

"Here's an application," Anita said in a pleasant tone. "Go ahead and fill it out. Then Mrs. Carson will speak with you."

Mrs. Carson.

Grace would be handling the interview? When Josie hatched the plan earlier that day she hadn't expected that.

Apprehension knotted her stomach. Flynt's mother was a kind, warmhearted soul, but she couldn't have been pleased with the way Josie had vanished last year.

"Something wrong?" asked the housekeeper.

"Oh, no. Nothing."

"Have a seat, then."

"Thanks."

The housekeeper left. Josie stared after her, wondering how long the woman had been working for the Carsons. Had they hired her right after Josie left—or had there been others before they found someone who worked out?

Well, whatever. Anita had the job now and she seemed pleasant and efficient. The Carsons were managing just fine without Josie Lavender to run their house for them.

Josie picked up one of the pens that waited in a mug on the table. It didn't take long to fill in all the blanks. A few minutes after she'd finished, Anita returned. She picked up the application. "This way, Ms. Lavender."

They went to the sitting room in Flynt's wing of the house. Grace was waiting by one of the high windows that looked out over a lush section of the garden. She turned as Josie and the housekeeper entered.

"Hello, Josie. So nice to see you." Grace's tone was warm. Her eyes were not. She crossed the room and took the application from the housekeeper. "Thank you, Anita."

The housekeeper nodded and backed out, pulling the double doors shut in front of her.

"Well," said Grace when they were alone. "Would you like anything? Coffee?"

"No, thanks."

"Have a seat." Grace gestured at a fiddle-back chair. Josie perched on the edge of it. Grace went around the coffee table and sat on the sofa.

The room had plum-colored walls trimmed in white. The furniture was big and fine and comfortable, the floors of dark, lustrous hardwood covered with beautiful Oriental rugs. It was just as Josie remembered it—and she remembered all too well.

Once, in a rage, a very pregnant Monica had grabbed a crystal vase from the marble-topped table in the corner and hurled it at Flynt. "I'm fat as one of your prize cows." She had called Flynt an ugly name. "It's your fault, and I hate you, Flynt Carson." And she'd let the vase fly. She hadn't even cared that the housekeeper happened to be in the room at the time.

Then, after Monica died, Flynt would sometimes drink himself to sleep in there. Not very often. He preferred his study for serious, all-night drinking. But now and then he would end up in the sitting room. More than once, Josie had come in to check on him and found him passed out on the sofa where Grace was sitting now. Josie would gently settle a blanket over him, her heart aching for him, loving him though she knew it was hopeless, calling herself a fool—and loving him anyway.

"So," said Grace, a little too brusquely for comfort, "I see you've been working at a day-care center."

"Yes. For nine months I was at Kid's Place Child Care up in Hurst. That's in the Fort—"

"I know where Hurst is, Josie."

Josie shut her mouth and looked down at her folded hands, feeling all of a sudden like a badly behaved young child. Grace Carson knew how to put you in your place with a gentle word and a reproving glance.

Grace said, "This is a glowing recommendation. They seem to have been very impressed with you."

Josie pulled herself up straight. "I loved working with the children. I had four months doing baby care, and then the rest of the time I had the toddlers." She had also worked nights as a waitress. With the two jobs, she'd been able to support herself in a modest way, to pay Flynt back the money she owed him, to buy her computer—and to send a little home to Alva, as well.

Grace sighed. "Josie." The papers in her hands rustled as she tightened her grip on them. "I think we'd better just get to the point here, don't you?"

Josie's stomach clenched all the harder. She kept her spine very straight. "Yes. Good idea."

"You…took off last year out of nowhere. One day you were here and we knew we could depend on you, and then you were gone. We never heard another word from you, until right now." Grace lifted one shoulder in a sad little shrug. "Oh, yes, Flynt did mention something about family difficulties. But that hardly made sense. We heard you had left town, left your mother behind." Grace hesitated, as if she couldn't decide how to go on.

Then she continued, "I'll admit, we were quite concerned for you at first. We thought that maybe your father...well, that he'd been released and you were frightened he might come after you.''

Josie's father had died in Huntsville Prison, ten months ago. Everyone in town knew that Josie had been the one to put him there.

Grace went on, ''But then we heard about what happened to him.'' Rutger Lavender had finally run into someone meaner than he was. He'd been stabbed in the prison yard by another inmate and died of the injury. ''So we knew that your father couldn't be the reason you left out of nowhere as you did.'' Grace sat back against the cushions and looked steadily at Josie, giving her the chance to come up with some sort of explanation.

Too bad she had none to give. Nothing she could say was going to make things any better. She would not tell Grace the truth—that she and Flynt had finally given in to the yearning that had grown too powerful for either of them to deny. They had given in and spent the night together in his bed. And then, the next morning, he had written her a check for ten thousand dollars and sent her away.

No, she wouldn't tell Grace that. She couldn't. And she refused to make up any lies.

Oh, what was she doing here? Obviously she had not thought this through. Assuming that Flynt would be handling the interviews, she'd had some crazy notion that he would simply hire her because she had showed up and applied for the job of caring for the baby he longed to believe was theirs.

"Well?" said Grace, the papers in her hands rustling some more as she shifted on the sofa. "I'd like to understand, Josie. I truly would, but—"

It wasn't going to work. It was a bad idea. Josie stood. "I'm sorry. I thought..."

"What?"

"Oh, it doesn't matter. I see now that I shouldn't have come. I—I do regret if I caused your family any hardship, leaving so suddenly the way that I did. All I can really tell you is that I had a good reason. But it was a private reason, one I just can't talk about."

Grace got to her feet. The coldness had left her eyes. "I'm sorry, too, Josie. You did a fine job for us. We had no complaints at all about the quality of your work." They looked at each other across the inlaid coffee table. "However, this is a helpless infant we're talking about now. I don't think it would be wise to hire someone we weren't certain we could count on one hundred percent."

Josie nodded. "It's all right. I understand."

"Understand what?" The deep voice came from over by the door.

A hot shiver skittered through Josie, a burning ripple of awareness sliding just below the surface of her skin. Flynt. He was a big man, but he could sure move quietly when he chose to. Josie hadn't heard him enter the room.

Apparently, neither had Grace. She put a hand to her throat. "Land sakes, Flynt Carson. What is it? Where's that baby? I thought you were—"

"Anita's got her. She's fine." He was answering Grace, but his eyes were on Josie. That blue gaze moved over her, measuring, judging. She felt that raking look right down into the center of her soul. "Anita mentioned that you were here."

Grace said, "Josie came to see about the nanny job."

He didn't even glance at his mother. "Yeah, Anita mentioned that, too."

Josie made herself smile and hoped it didn't look too forced. She wished he'd stop staring at her. She'd kept her mouth shut about the two of them, but keeping quiet wouldn't help if he was going to stare at her like that with his mama standing right there, looking on.

"Yes," Josie said carefully. "But it hasn't... worked out. I was just leaving." She started to move for the door, hoping against hope that he'd simply move out of her way.

So much for her hopes.

He came striding toward her, the look in his eye freezing her in her tracks. He didn't stop until he was standing right in front of her. "Stay. We'll talk."

Grace was looking worried. "Flynt, honey, Josie said she's leaving. I think we ought to just let her—"

He cut her off with a movement of his arm—a

gesture toward the papers Grace held clutched in her fist. "Is that her application?"

"Well, yes, and a reference, but—"

"Let me see them."

"Flynt—"

He held out his hand. Grace gave in and passed him the papers. "Thanks, Ma. Go on and relieve Anita, will you?"

"But—"

"I'll handle this." He had that look. Josie recognized it and she was sure his mother did, too. It was the look that said he would do what he meant to do. Nothing—and no one—was going to talk him out of it.

Grace nodded, the slightest downward tipping of her round chin. She knew her own son well enough to see when she couldn't win. "Josie," she said quietly, "it *is* good to see that you are well."

"Thank you, Mrs. Carson. I'm pleased that you found another housekeeper who seems to be working out."

Grace nodded again and then slid around the end of the coffee table and left the room. Flynt let her get through the doors, then he spun on his heel and went to make certain they were both firmly shut. Josie waited where he'd left her, staring down at the rug beneath her feet, her pulse racing so fast and hard it made a rushing sound in her ears.

She should tell him, firmly, to open the doors. That

she was leaving. That she'd made up her mind. Coming here had not been wise.

But she only went on, head down like some shy little miss, staring at the roses twining in the rug, thinking that this was what she'd wanted, wasn't it? That this was why she'd come.

She watched his fine, tooled boots come at her. They stopped not two feet from her chunky-heeled black shoes.

He dropped the papers onto the coffee table and then he spoke very softly, for her ears alone. "Okay, Josie. You have something to tell me?"

She made herself look up. He was wearing blue jeans and a slightly faded Western shirt. He smelled of that tempting, expensive aftershave he always wore, and of saddle soap. He'd probably been out riding earlier in the day. Unlike Matt, who was the real cowboy in the family, Flynt dressed like a businessman more often than not. He ran the family interests, while Matt saw to the day-to-day workings of the ranch itself.

Josie's glance stopped at the top snap of his shirt. Somehow, she couldn't bring herself to look into those eyes of his right then.

He whispered her name, putting a question mark at the end of it.

Something in his tone did it. She was able to raise her head and look into his face.

"Well?" He put those hands of his on her shoulders oh-so-gently.

Her knees turned to water. She wanted only to sway against him, feel the heat and hardness of him. Oh, she had missed him. They'd only shared that one night, and that had been eleven months ago, eleven months that felt like forever—and somehow, at the same time, like just yesterday. He was smiling, the most tender, gentle smile. "It's all right," he told her. "I'll stand with you. I promise you. I just need the truth from you, and we can start to figure out how to handle all this."

She blinked. "How to...?" And then she understood.

He thought she had come to confess about the baby.

She had to press her lips together or else she would have burst out into a wild-woman shout of hysterical laughter. He just wouldn't get it. Wouldn't listen. He wasn't a stupid man, but on this subject you would have thought he had a block of wood for a brain.

Some of her agitation must have shown on her face, or maybe he felt her stiffen under his hands. "Shh," he said soothingly, in the way a man would gentle a spooked horse. "It's okay, settle down."

"Flynt."

"Go ahead. You can say it. Just say the truth and we can go on from here."

"Flynt, please."

"Josie—"

"No." She stepped back. He resisted letting her go, but only briefly. Then he caught himself and dropped his hands to his sides. She said, slowly and clearly, "I didn't come here to tell you that the baby is mine. I can't tell you that, Flynt. Because she is not mine."

He was the one who stepped back then, leaving a yawning chasm between them. The tender look in his eyes had vanished. His jaw was set.

"Not yours," he said flatly and with no belief at all.

"That's right. Not mine. Not *ours.*"

"Hell, Josie." He blew out a weary breath.

She wanted to scream and jump up and down and call him a thousand kinds of pigheaded fool. But she controlled herself somehow. She spoke slowly, carefully, reasonably. "I am not a liar, Flynt. I'm not a woman who will do something and then say I never did. I'll keep my mouth shut, maybe. I'll skirt the truth now and then. But I'm not going to lie bald-faced over and over. You know I'm not that kind."

He looked away, then back. "Even the most honest people will lie when they have to, when they feel they've got no other choice."

"Flynt, look at me. Look in my face." She waited until his eyes were burning into hers. "I think a big part of what you've always liked about me—and you do like me, don't you?''

''What kind of question is that?''

''A straight one. I'm not talkin' about wanting, about whatever it is that makes our hearts beat too fast when we get near each other. I'm just talking about respect. About one person liking how another person is. And I'm asking, do you like me?''

''Damn it, Josie.''

''Do you?''

''Yes. Yes, I like you. You know I do.''

''That's right. I do know. And I know why, too. You like me because I'm strong and I'm straight. Because I've been through a lot and things haven't always been so good for me, but I'm still standing. I'm still keeping on, doing the right thing as best I can—and not usin' any drugs or alcohol to soften the edges of how hard life can be. My daddy was a messed up, wife-abusing drunk. And you know and everyone knows that I am the reason he ended up in prison. I called the police on him and I testified against him so they could put him away where he belonged. In spite of all of that, I got through high school with a three-point-six GPA and someday, the good Lord willing, I'll get a college education. I ran this whole big house of yours before I was twenty years old. I moved up to Hurst when you sent me away and I worked hard and I paid you back every penny you gave to me.

"I may be more than ten years younger than you, but that doesn't make me weak and helpless. Not by a long shot. I don't know what I would have done if I'd had your baby. I can't talk about what never was. Because that baby you found on the golf course is not mine. And I think, if you'd only be honest with yourself, that you know she's not mine."

He looked at her sideways. "If she's not yours, then what are you doing here?"

Josie felt tired then, tired right down to her bones. It was no good. No matter how hard she tried, she wasn't getting through to him.

"I said, what are you doing here?"

"Your mama told you. I came to apply for the nanny job."

"Why—if Lena isn't yours?"

"Because I love babies and someone has to take care of that poor little girl. And because—" She stopped herself, not sure if she really wanted to reveal the rest.

"What?"

She made herself say it. "Because I still have hope. I still...want a chance with you."

"A chance." His tone made it achingly clear that she didn't have a prayer in the world for such a thing.

She sighed then. "That's right. God knows why, but it's true. I still want a chance to make things work with you."

"There is no chance with me. You know that."

She shook her head and then spoke with some anger. "Not unless that baby is ours, right? Then you'd have to do the right thing, wouldn't you?" She dared to step up next to him again, to tip her head back and speak right into his grim, set face. "For the sake of that baby, you'd put aside that awful promise you made to yourself when Monica died."

He didn't even blink. "So?"

"Am I right?"

"You just said the baby wasn't ours."

"You aren't answering my question, Flynt."

"Is Lena ours?"

"How many times do I have to say it?"

"This once. Answer now and I won't ask you again."

"Is this some kind of a deal you're offering? I say it one more time, and you'll believe me, you'll finally let it go?"

"Let's put it this way. I'll stop asking."

She saw what he was getting at. "So, you won't believe me, you just won't ask again. You'll wait for the results of that paternity test."

"You can volunteer the truth anytime between now and then."

"Oh, well, thank you. Thank you so much."

"No call for sarcasm, Josie."

"Not from where you're standing, maybe."

"Is Lena ours?"

"No. She is not."

"Well," he said. "Okay, then. Fair enough."

"What in the world has 'fair' got to do with it?"

He ignored the question and asked another one of his own. "You still want the job of taking care of her?"

She realized her mouth had dropped open and snapped it shut. "You're offering it to me?"

"That's right. You'll have to move in here."

"I…yes, that's what the ad in the *Clarion* said."

"You'll get two days off—the weekend—Friday at 6:00 p.m. to the same time on Sunday. But other than that, you'll be with Lena pretty much round-the-clock—well, except for, say, three hours a day, Monday through Thursday. How's that? Let's say from two to five in the afternoon as a rule. I'll spell you, or my mother will, or Cara—school's out now, so she's available in the daytime now and then." Cara was a teacher at Mission Creek High. "So you'll be able to check on Alva, make sure she's got everything she needs and she's doing all right."

"But—"

"The money will be good." He named a figure.

He was right. It was very good. After working in day care, Josie knew what such jobs generally paid, and it wasn't a third of what Flynt had just offered. The hours would be much longer, true. But she'd get her room and board in the deal.

"You'll have to talk to the people at the café, tell them you're quitting. I need you to start right away."

"Wait a minute. Your mother already as good as said she wouldn't hire me."

"My mother isn't making this decision. Do you want the job?"

Lord help her. "Yes," she said. "I do."

Six

The room off Flynt's bedroom had become a nursery again. Josie recognized all the cute white-painted furniture stenciled with dancing teddy bears holding big, bright balloons. The bins of baby toys were back. So were the open shelves stacked with soft receiving blankets and sweet little snap-front T-shirts and pastel rompers.

Flynt had even had someone in to paint fresh murals on the walls. Now it was fairies hovering in the air and cute, goofy-looking frogs in a pond. Before, it had been more teddy bears and a big rainbow arching across the ceiling.

The baby lay on a play mat, on the soft dark-green carpet, waving her fat little arms and making giggly sounds at the toys dangling from the play station set up above her. Grace was sitting in a rocker a few feet away. She had an open book in her lap, but she was watching the child, a soft smile on her mouth, looking as fond as a doting grandmother—which she probably felt certain she was. She took off her reading glasses when Flynt led Josie into the room, the soft smile becoming a flat line, the faint wrinkles in her brow etching deeper than before. Josie read her expression. Grace knew that Lena's nanny had been hired and she did not in the least approve of her son's choice.

Her book had one of those ribbon markers hooked to the spine. Grace smoothed it in to save her place, shut the book and stood. "Well," she said. And that was all. She waited for Flynt to tell her what she already knew.

Flynt didn't make her wait long. "Josie's taking the nanny job, Ma."

"I see." Grace gave her son a tiny smile—just the slightest upward tilting at the edges of her mouth. It was the smile of a trueborn lady. So polite. So cool. So very disapproving. She turned that itty-bitty smile on Josie. "Josie, could you wait in the sitting room for a minute or two, so that Flynt and I might have a word alone?"

Josie didn't even think to argue. "Of course." She started to turn.

Flynt stopped her with a hand on her arm.

Josie flinched at the contact. She stared into those eyes of his. Her arm burned where he held it, his flesh to hers.

"Stay here."

"But—"

He just looked at her.

She found herself nodding. "Yes, all right."

He released her. "Ma, it's decided. Josie's going home to get her things, to check on Alva and quit her other job. Starting tonight, she'll be looking after Lena five days a week.''

''I see,'' Grace said again, that itty-bitty ladylike smile never wavering. She knew her son, knew when even her considerable powers of persuasion weren't going to be enough to make him see things her way. ''Well, then, what can I say? If the decision is made…''

''It is. Josie will take the spare room next door.''

Next door, Josie thought, warmth pooling in her belly. There'll be my room and then the baby's room and then his room.

On the floor, the baby let out a particularly high-spirited giggle. Josie looked down at her—and never wanted to look away. Oh, what a precious little darling she was, with those feathery midnight curls and those wide eyes. To have a baby like that in her arms would almost make this mess she was getting herself into bearable.

Because Josie had few illusions. Coming back to work here wouldn't be any picnic. Flynt was a difficult man, to put it mildly. And Grace clearly didn't want her here. Who could say what the rest of the Carsons would think of Josie Lavender living in their house again?

However, she would have this baby to hold and to cherish, to pamper and fuss over. And yes, to love.

Except for Lena's little coos and sighs, the room

had fallen silent. Josie looked up to find both Flynt and Grace watching her.

Well, fine. Let them stare. "Do you mind if I...?"

"You're the nanny." There was something in Flynt's voice. Triumph, maybe. Or vindication. "Go ahead."

Josie was across the room and kneeling before that little sweetheart in two seconds flat. "Oh, look at you. You're a happy girl, aren't you? A sweet, beautiful, happy little girl."

The baby blinked those gorgeous blue eyes and looked right at Josie. Then she made one of those baby sounds that almost might have been actual words.

Josie couldn't help chuckling. "I think she just said, 'You bet.'"

"You want to hold her, don't you?" Flynt made the question into something very close to a taunt.

Josie decided not to rise to the bait. "I sure do," she said honestly.

"No one's stopping you."

Josie moved the play station and gathered that little darling into her arms. Lena giggled some more—and then rested her silky dark head on Josie's shoulder. Josie kissed the black curls and patted the tiny back. When she turned, she found both Flynt and his mother still staring at her.

She decided to ignore them. She rocked the baby gently from side to side and indulged herself in a few more little kisses—on that satin-soft cheek, on the perfect shell of a small, warm ear.

At last, Grace turned to her son and asked a little stiffly, "Do you want me to stay with her until Josie can get her things and come back?"

"I'd appreciate it. I've got a few calls to make."

"No problem." Grace set her book on the small table by the rocker and held out her arms.

Reluctantly Josie handed Lena over. "I'll probably be two or three hours."

"It's all right," said Grace, holding Lena close. "We'll manage just fine."

Alva was lying on the sofa, as usual, when Josie got home. But she looked pretty good. Her oxygen was turned off and wheeled over into the corner. Day by day, the circles beneath her eyes seemed a little lighter, her cheeks a little less pale.

She sat up. "Josie, honey, I'm thinking maybe I'll fix us both some macaroni and cheese. I know you love macaroni and cheese."

Josie sat down beside her and took her hand. "Mama…"

Alva looked at her with a mother's knowing eyes. "Something's happened. What?"

"Well, it's kind of a sudden thing, I know, but I've been offered a nanny job out at Carson Ranch."

"Just now? Today?"

"That's right."

"A nanny job…watching the mystery baby?"

"Mama. How'd you know about the mystery baby?"

"I may be under the weather lately, but I have a few friends in town. And I've also got a phone."

"Everybody's talking, huh?"

"Aren't they always?"

"Yeah, I suppose they are." Josie rubbed the back of Alva's thin, wrinkled hand. Her mother was only forty-five. But judging by her hands, she might have been seventy or more. "Mama…"

"Spit it out, now, sweetie."

"Well, it's a round-the-clock job. I would have to stay at the ranch five days a week. I'd come home every day, though, to check on you and I'd have two days off."

"You talked to Gus over at the café yet?"

Josie shook her head. "I'll go see him next."

"Oh, don't look so serious." Alva's smile was a little wan, but it was a smile, nonetheless. "You know Gus. He'll holler some and then he'll say as soon as you want your job back, you got it."

Josie nodded. "I have to admit that does sound like Gus."

"He knows a hard worker when he's got one. This nanny job pay good?"

"Very good."

"And you want to do it?"

"Yes. I do."

Her mother reached out, brushed a few strands of hair out of Josie's eyes. "And not only for the money, am I right?"

"Oh, Mama…" All at once, there were tears pushing at the back of her throat.

"What, now? What is makin' you cry?"

"I'm not crying. Not quite, anyway."

"Tell me. Come on."

"Well, when it comes to love and all that, I only wanted to find a good man, you know? A nice, stable, solid kind of guy."

"Who is it?"

Her mother's sudden question took Josie by surprise. "What?"

"Oh, honey, I always suspected there was someone at that house when you were working there before— and then, when you quit all of a sudden and decided to head up to Dallas, I knew something was wrong. You had that look of a woman brokenhearted, but you weren't talkin'."

Josie patted Alva's hand some more. "I didn't want to worry you."

"You'll worry me more now by not telling me who the man is."

Josie swallowed. Why not tell her mother? Alva only wanted to understand. "It's Flynt Carson."

"Oh, my," said Alva, shaking her head.

"Keep it to yourself, Mama."

"Don't you worry. I will."

"I can see it in your eyes. You think I'm making a big mistake."

"It's all right," her mama said. "You follow your heart now. You're wiser than I ever was. And your heart does know the way."

Josie didn't get back to the ranch until after seven. Cara was watching Lena by then.

"Josie." Cara had kind eyes—eyes that made no judgments. "We've missed you. Good to have you back."

"Good to be here." And it was—though it was a little bit nerve-racking, too. She kept thinking how she'd be sleeping right down the hall from Flynt. And taking care of the baby he still believed to be theirs.

"You'll need time to put your things away," Cara suggested. "I'll stay here with Lena. Go ahead and get settled in."

"Thanks."

Cara waved a hand as if to say that thanks weren't needed. "What about dinner? Did you eat? Call the kitchen and have something sent to your room."

Josie spent a half an hour or so putting some of her clothes into drawers and hanging the rest in her new room's small closet. She also set out the few personal things she liked to have with her wherever she stayed—a framed picture of herself and Alva, a little chipped Hummel statue of a shepherd boy holding a lamb, some big quartz crystals she'd found on a trip to Arkansas and, of course, her computer.

The housekeeper brought up her tray just as she got everything in order. She carried it into the baby's room, thinking she'd tell Cara it was okay if she wanted to go.

But Cara had already slipped out, probably gone home to the small caretaker's cottage not far from the main house, where she'd lived since before Josie first came to work for the Carson family. Josie entered the nursery room to find Flynt bending over Lena's crib.

He straightened and turned to her. He'd changed his clothes since that afternoon. Now he wore gray slacks and a dress shirt the same color as his eyes. It almost hurt to look at him, he was so handsome.

Heartbreaker, she thought, and wondered again at the wisdom of returning here.

"Everything all right?" he asked.

She frowned. "All right?"

"Your room. Is it all right? Did you find everything you need?"

"It's great." She thought of her computer. "There's a desk in there, and I'm glad about that. But there is one thing…"

"Name it."

"About the phone…"

"Right. Works like an office phone. If you pick it up, it buzzes Anita and the kitchen. If you want to dial out, just dial 9 first."

"Well, I figured that out. Problem is, I have a phone modem for my computer and—"

He didn't let her get the whole sentence out. "Cable modem's better. I'll see you get a line in there first thing tomorrow."

"There's no need for that. I've got a server. It's all set up. All I need is—"

"Josie, take my word. You'll be happier with high-speed service."

She opened her mouth to argue further and then decided against it. Why not just take the cable hookup, since he was offering one? She'd still have her server, if she needed it later—if this crazy scheme of hers to give the two of them another chance together didn't work out. "All right. Thanks."

Because Lena was fussing a little, Flynt lifted her from the crib. He carried her over to the bureau/changing table, laid her down and checked her diaper.

"Wet," he said, bending so close his forehead and Lena's almost met.

"Oog. Ga," said Lena.

"Yes, ma'am," Flynt replied. "I'm on it." And he was. In no time at all, he was snapping her back into her lightweight pj's. "There. All better." Lena let out more nonsense sounds, waving her arms and kicking her legs. Her fat little fist ran into his nose, then opened and grabbed on.

"Hey." He laughed, catching that tiny hand, which

instantly wrapped itself around his thumb. "Cut it out." He kissed the plump pink knuckles.

Josie looked on, her poor heart melting right down to pure mush. He did have a way with that baby, now, didn't he? And he didn't even flinch at the prospect of changing a diaper.

Heartbreaker, he might be. But there was good-guy potential there, a steady, dependable man inside him. Always had been.

Josie's job over the next two weeks or so—until the results of that paternity test came through and the unassailable truth finally had to be faced—would be to set that good man free.

He slid a clean diaper onto his shoulder and then lifted Lena into his arms.

Right then he looked at Josie and scowled. "What?" The word was pure challenge. He must have seen the softness in her eyes.

She almost lied, almost waved a hand and told him nothing.

But where would avoiding his challenges get her?

Hey, she thought. I've quit my job and gone and moved in down the hall from him. Might as well go for it, starting right now.

She asked, "How in the world did you ever get it in your head to marry someone like Monica?"

Seven

Flynt had a little trouble believing she'd said that.

He didn't like to talk about Monica, and everyone close to him knew it. Josie knew it. She knew it damn well.

People respected his natural desire for silence on the subject of Monica. They respected his grief and they knew of his guilt.

They left it alone.

Josie had always left it alone, too—at least, until now. It wasn't as if she didn't already know plenty. She'd seen way too much, both of the hell that his marriage had been and after, when he tried to drown himself in a river of good scotch.

"Flynt?"

He didn't answer. He turned from her and carried Lena back to her crib, laid her down. Those innocent eyes looked up at him, that little mouth moving, hand still waving.

Behind him, Josie said nothing.

Damn her.

It wasn't the first time she'd presumed more than she should have with him.

She was the one, after all, who had shamed him into getting sober a year and a half ago. She'd told him off good and proper, when no one else had the guts to do it.

Shocked the hell out of him, when she did that.

Josie, of all people. Josie, who looked after him, who took care of him, who kept her mouth shut and her eyes down.

For a year or so after the accident, she'd coddled him. There was no other word for it. She'd help him stagger to his bedroom late at night when he was still just sober enough to get there before he passed out. And when he passed out before he got there, she'd take off his shoes and put a blanket over him. She'd clean up his messes.

For that year, she gave him just what he needed in a woman: a combination nanny and servant. She had the patience of a saint. If someone had told him ahead of time that it was his housekeeper who would finally get him to put the cork in the bottle, he'd have laughed them right out of Texas.

People did try in that year to talk to him about his drinking. His mother had come after him, and his father. They'd even sent Judge Bridges in one day to try to make him see the light.

He'd ignored them all and kept on drinking.

And then, a year and a half ago, in December, Josie came into his study one morning when he was still passed out at his desk and she pulled all the curtains wide-open, letting in the hard, clear light of day. He'd groaned, growled at her to get out, and then turned his head away from the light.

He hadn't bargained on her bringing a bucket of ice water with her. She threw it on him.

He came out of that desk chair bellowing, calling her a number of very bad names. He grabbed for her—and she slapped him, hard.

And then she started talking.

She told him off good and proper for throwing his life away. She called him a coward. She said he had no right at all to treat his body that way. She said he was hurting not only himself, but everyone who cared about him, by carrying on the way he was.

She said it was time he quit rolling around in his own self-pity. That he had to pick himself up off the floor and get on with his life.

Somehow, when Josie told him off, it worked. He hadn't had a drink since that December morning.

And she'd gone back to doing her job. They hardly spoke, except for the kind of things that pass between a man and a member of his household staff.

"Coffee, Mr. Carson?"

"Yeah—by the way, did you pick up those shirts?"

"They're in your closet."

"Great, Josie. Thanks."

But he was more aware of her than before. He felt the tension building between them. He noticed things he shouldn't: that she had pretty, slim hands with long, graceful fingers. That her neck was white and smooth and seemed to beg to have his mouth on it. That she had breasts just the right size to fill his hands...

And then came that night in July. It was a week-night, the twelfth. The day had been a scorcher.

He'd arrived home from a series of meetings and property tours in Corpus. It was after eight and he went straight to the air-conditioned comfort of his own rooms, not pausing to greet anyone in the family. He wanted a drink. Since that wasn't an option, he'd reconciled himself to settling for some food and some peace and quiet, followed by a shower and a good night's sleep. He'd ordered a tray sent up to his study.

He was there, at his desk—the same desk she'd splattered with ice water six months before—when Josie brought him the tray. He had his laptop open and he was studying some drawings for prospective additions to one of the family's apartment complexes.

She entered quietly, as always. She could move into a room, do whatever needed doing there and leave again with no one the wiser. But in his study, the desk faced the door. He saw her come in.

He knew he should tell her to put the tray down on the low table across the room. But when he opened his mouth, the wrong thing came out.

"I'd like it over here, Josie." He indicated a clear spot on his desk.

She came toward him, her head down just a little, not making eye contact, looking at the tray as if she didn't dare *not* look at it.

She reached his side. He smelled the clean, dewy scent of her. She put the tray down right next to him.

Before she could slide silently away, he caught her hand—just reached out and snared it—and held on way too tight.

She gasped. Then she met his eyes and whispered his name. ''Flynt?''

He was up out of the chair, yanking her into his arms, pulling her as close as he'd been dreaming he might get her and bringing his mouth down to taste hers, at last....

In the crib, the way babies will, Lena had dropped off to sleep. She simply shut her eyes and in one split second she went off to dreamland, her little mouth slightly open.

Behind him, Josie remained silent.

He had to hand it to her. The woman had nerves of steel to stick there the way she was, saying nothing, waiting for the moment when he'd have to turn and deal with her.

He gave in, straightening and turning to face her. ''I don't like to talk about Monica.''

''I know.''

He let an endless minute or two go by before he

spoke again. "I met her on a business trip to Atlanta."

"Yes. I heard that somewhere. That she was from Atlanta."

"Is there anything you *haven't* heard?" He spoke roughly.

She refused to be put in her place by his tone. "Yep," she replied downright cheerfully. "I never heard why you married her."

"So you asked."

"That's right."

He probably should have told her to mind her own business and turned and left her there to do the job he'd hired her for. But he didn't.

"You saw her. All that black hair, those pale eyes and that white, white skin. And a Waverly. The Waverlys are a very important family in Atlanta." There was a butterfly mobile over Lena's crib. He tapped it and the butterflies danced. "Monica was an only child, pampered, thoroughly self-absorbed."

"Just your type, huh?"

He sent her a lowering look. "I'll pretend you didn't say that."

She dared to shrug. "Suit yourself."

He turned to her fully, folding his arms across his chest. "What happened to the quiet, unassuming housekeeper I used to know?"

Her gaze did not waver. "I'm not your housekeeper anymore."

"No. Now you're the nanny."

She shrugged again. And she waited for him to go on.

He went ahead and obliged her. "Let's see. Why did I marry Monica? Well, for all the wrong reasons, obviously. Because she was beautiful. I really liked the way she danced, the way she laughed, the way all the other men wanted her. *I* wanted her. You could say I was…dazzled by her, I suppose. She was a prize to be won. I wanted to bring her home and show her off. One of the Atlanta Waverlys. My wife."

"Are you saying that you never loved her?"

"Love." He gave the word back to her, his ambivalence about it clear in his tone.

"What does that mean? Did you love her or not?"

"All right. Yeah, I loved her—or at least I thought at the time that what I felt for her was love. But looking back, with all the wisdom hindsight affords…" He let the thought finish itself.

Josie said, "Well, I did get the picture that you wanted to start a family and she didn't. That always seemed to be a problem between you."

Denials rose to his lips. He didn't voice them. They would have been lies and Josie would have recognized them as such. After all, Monica had never been the quiet type. Whatever was on her mind came right out of her mouth. Josie had heard it all, especially after Monica finally got pregnant. Monica had hated watching her figure go and her ankles swell and she'd made no secret of her feelings.

"I was ready for a family. Or at least, I thought I was. I'd been to college, been a soldier and a prisoner of war. Came back a hero—and then got myself in that big, ugly mess when Haley Mercado drowned." He looked at her measuringly. "You know all about Haley Mercado, right?"

"Well, Flynt, I do read the newspapers."

"It was our fault. Mine, Luke Callaghan's, Tyler Murdoch's and Spence Harrison's."

"Wait a minute. The way I remember it, they found all four of you *not* guilty, at the trial."

"Carl Bridges got us off. That doesn't mean we weren't at fault. We were heroes home from the war. We were very drunk and very full of ourselves. We goaded Haley into going on a midnight boat ride on Lake Maria with us. The boat capsized and we all went under. Haley never resurfaced."

"It was an accident."

"She shouldn't have been in that boat. She *wouldn't* have been in that boat. We razzed her like hell until she finally went with us."

Josie studied him from across the room, her pose a mirror of his, arms folded over those beautiful breasts. "You're way too guilty about too many things."

"Maybe I have a lot to be guilty about."

"Everybody has a lot to be guilty about. It's called

being human. You pick yourself up off the floor and you try again. You do better the next time.''

''Oh?''

She dipped her head in a nod. ''Yeah.'' A lock of that white-blond hair of hers drifted over her shoulder. She lifted a hand and guided it out of the way behind her ear.

He wanted to do that—to be able to reach out and smooth her hair, to run a finger over the silky skin of her soft cheek. To cross the room, right now, and reach for her. To pull her close and—

He cut off the thought before it could get too dangerous. He didn't have the right to touch her.

Not yet. In a couple of weeks, maybe.

But for now...

''Any more 'whys' for me tonight, Josie?''

''Hmm,'' she said, as if the question required serious consideration. Then she smiled. ''No. I think that'll do it for now. You can go.''

The cable people came at ten the next morning to install the line for Josie's Internet connection. It always surprised her how fast a thing could get done when a Carson gave the order for it.

By that evening she had everything all set up. Her room's one window looked out on a pretty, sheltered section of the garden. She put the desk there. When Lena didn't need her, she could be at the computer, writing in the journal she kept on disk, playing games and continuing her e-mail correspondence with a few friends she'd made at the day-care center and in that waitress job she'd had while she lived in Hurst.

It would be nice sometimes simply to sit there at the window and read a book—she'd always liked to read. And then she had those three hours a day for going to her mother's and making sure Alva had everything she needed.

The nanny job would be fine. She'd keep busy even in the quiet times when Lena was napping.

That whole first day Josie was aware of a kind of edgy, excited feeling, as if there were a thousand tiny butterflies trapped just under her skin, waiting for a certain signal to begin beating their wings.

The signal being Flynt Carson's presence, of course.

The night before had raised her hopes a little. He had, after all, answered more or less honestly when she'd asked about Monica. She kept imagining more conversations in the same vein. She would get him to open up about himself, and she would share with him all the secrets of her heart.

By the time he got the results of that paternity test, those results wouldn't matter. He'd have realized that the two of them were meant to spend their lives side by side.

Josie didn't see him that whole day. He was most likely off empire building or out playing cowboy, getting his hands dirty with real ranch work alongside Matt.

Cara appeared to relieve her when the time came to check on Alva. Three hours later, when Josie returned to the ranch, she ran into Flynt's father in the back hall. Ford Carson was dressed in work clothes, with manure on his boots.

"Hello, Josie," he said in that deep, rather gruff voice of his, thick white eyebrows drawn together, eyes narrowed, as if he wanted to check inside her head and make sure there was nothing suspicious going on in there. Josie had always thought of Flynt's father as a fair and good-natured man, a man who loved his wife and seemed pretty happy with how his life had turned out. The probing way he looked at her now made her feel more than a little bit nervous.

Josie put on a friendly smile. "Nice to see you, Mr. Carson."

"How have you been?"

"Just fine."

"Glad to hear it. I understand you'll be taking care of little Lena for us."

"Yes, that's right."

"Good, then." He went on looking at her in that odd, intent way. She had the distinct impression he wanted to say something to her but didn't quite know where to start. "Well," he said, finally, gruffer than ever, "you've just been to see your mother, I suppose?"

"Yes."

"She's okay?"

"She's fine."

"All right. I hope…things are working out."

"Things are just fine."

"Glad to hear that. Yes. Real good."

Josie hurried to her own room to drop off a few purchases she'd made for herself when she stopped at the store to shop for her mother. Then she ducked into the bathroom to wash her hands.

Finally she entered the baby's room to find that Grace had taken over for Cara.

Grace turned a cool smile on Josie. "Ah, there you are."

"Am I late?"

"No. You're right on time."

Grace let the smile fade. Without it, she looked vaguely put-upon, as if Josie had injured her or insulted her somehow.

But a lady was a lady, after all. Grace couldn't stop herself from asking, "How is your mother doing, Josie?"

"Better, Mrs. Carson. Better all the time." Yes, all right. The improvement, according to the doctors, was most likely only temporary. But Grace Carson didn't need to hear the depressing details.

Grace stood from the rocker, slowly, careful of the baby in her arms. "You give her my very best, will you?"

"I sure will. And thank you."

"Josie, I..."

Josie waited, wearing an expression of polite attention, for Flynt's mother to find the right words.

At last, they came. "You know, you've got your whole life before you. You're young. Quite lovely. And I know you're very bright."

In Josie's experience, when people felt a need to start out by listing your good points, bad news was sure to follow. She didn't like the sound of this. She ventured a cautious, "Thank you."

Grace gave a tight little nod. "You must have boyfriends, social activities you hate to miss. I would think this kind of job would be so...limiting for you."

Josie caught on then. Grace *knew*. She'd picked up on the tension between the housekeeper-turned-nanny and her older son. She might not know how far it had gone, but she did know now that an attraction existed.

And she didn't approve.

Suddenly that narrow-eyed look of Ford's in the back hall made a bleak kind of sense. He'd wanted to talk to her, all right.

He'd wanted to tell her to stay away from his son.

What had she expected? For them to throw open their arms and beg her to join the family?

Yes, some very young, hopeful voice in the back of her mind whispered ardently. *Yes, I did expect that.*

"You'll be here, in these two rooms, so much of the time." Grace clucked her tongue. "I can't believe you'll be happy, with only this baby for company day in and day out.''

Josie kept her shoulders back and her head high. ''Mrs. Carson, I told you yesterday in the interview, I love babies. And I'm good with them. I will be happy alone with Lena. And as far as all those other things you mentioned, well, in my life there hasn't been a lot of time for boyfriends and partying.''

''There should be.''

''*Should* doesn't mean a lot to me. There's what is. And there's what I'll make of what life has handed to me. That's about it.''

''I think you should consider carefully.'' There it was—another *should*. Grace didn't even seem to realize she'd said it. She went on, ''Ford and I would be willing to—''

Josie put up a hand. ''Please don't say anything we'll both regret later.''

One of Grace's slim eyebrows inched toward her hairline. ''Pardon me?''

''Let me put it this way. If you had some idea of making me an offer to just go away again… Well, I wouldn't take it and we'd both always know that you had made it. So we'd both be better off if you never offered and I never knew for sure that you meant to.''

Grace's hand, gently stroking Lena's feathery curls, went still. ''You know, Josie, it's possible that you are a little too smart for your own good.''

Too smart for her own good.

It was what her daddy used to say to her—usually just before he whacked her upside the head. Josie had always wanted to talk right back to him, to tell him that yes, she was very smart. Smarter than he was, for certain. And that brains, no matter what some folks would like a girl to believe, were a blessing and she was proud to have them.

Josie considered saying that very thing to Grace Carson right then. But she didn't. She also had a big urge to just get it all out there, to tell Flynt's mother proudly that yes, it was true. She *was* after the Carson's precious older son and before she gave up this time around, she planned to put up one hell of a fight.

But what would saying something like that accomplish? What she and Flynt had or didn't have together was between the two of them. His family had to be secondary. The Carsons' disappointing attitude toward Josie would be a problem only if there was a relationship in the first place.

Right now, well, there wasn't much more than a powerful yearning that eleven months apart hadn't done a thing to kill.

"I'd imagine there's not much more to say right now, is there?"

"No, Mrs. Carson. I guess there's not."

Grace handed her the baby and left, and Josie did her best to put their conversation from her mind.

* * *

Flynt finally appeared in the baby's room at a little after nine. Josie was just snapping Lena back into her sleeper after a diaper change.

"Here," he said. "Let me hold her."

Her silly heart going a mile a minute in pure gladness at the sight of him, Josie lifted the baby from the changing pad and passed her over.

He put the little darling on his shoulder—and turned his back to Josie. "Go ahead. Take a break."

She stared at those broad shoulders, at the back of his head. Dismissed, she thought. I am dismissed— and after spending a whole day looking forward to seeing him. Not to mention after his mama almost offered me money to saddle up and get the heck out of Dodge.

He turned then, in time to catch her crossing her eyes and sticking out her tongue at him. He blinked— and then he let out a laugh of pure surprise. That got her laughing, too.

Too bad he grew serious again so darn fast. "Josie, listen…"

She composed her expression. "All right. What?"

"We've got to watch it."

"What, exactly, is 'it'?"

"You know what."

She did, of course. "Maybe *you* think we should watch it. I don't happen to agree with you."

He turned from her again—but only to put Lena in

her crib. Then he faced her once more. "We can't be around each other too much. You've got to...keep your distance."

"Why?"

He rubbed the back of his neck, as if the muscles there pained him. "You sure are full of 'whys' lately."

"Well, maybe I am. Maybe it's time someone asked 'why' now and then, instead of just blindly letting things go on as they are. Things aren't so good as they are. Or maybe you haven't noticed."

"Things are the way they are. They're not going to change."

"That's right. They won't. Not if you don't let them."

"It's not a matter of 'letting.'"

There was too much space between them. She decided to fix that. She took a step toward him, and another.

"Stop, Josie. Stay right there."

"Why, Flynt Carson, you are afraid of me."

He muttered a low curse.

She smiled. "Swearing is not going to save you." She backed him against the baby's crib and she got right up to him, right in his face.

His hungry gaze met hers, then slid lower to lock on her mouth. "Back off, Josie."

"No, I will not. But you are lots bigger than me. I think you can get away—if you really want to."

She waited, giving him the chance to get clear of her if he meant to. He didn't move. The warmth of him was all around her. The air seemed to hum and shimmer between them.

She said, "Things are going to change, Flynt Carson. I'm going to see to it."

"No." The word sounded wrung out of him.

"Yes."

"Josie..." It was a plea.

She showed no mercy. She pressed herself against him—oh, it felt just wonderful, to be this close to him again—and she tipped up her mouth for him to take.

Desire hung on a thread for an endless second or two.

And then, with a desperate moan, he yanked her close and lowered his mouth to cover hers.

Eight

Flynt's mind kept giving orders: Stop. Let her go. Pull away. *Now.*

But the rest of him refused to listen.

He had her in his arms. Her sweet mouth was open under his. Her soft hands clutched his shoulders, all the captivating curves and hollows of her pressing against him, promising him everything—what he longed for, what he couldn't forget, what he was never again to have.

Unless...

He pulled his mouth from hers—not far, just enough that he could say what needed saying into her beautiful, flushed face. "Josie, admit it. Admit it now. Say that Lena is—"

She slid a soft hand between them, covering his lips. "No," she whispered, her eyes so tender, the single word weighted with passionate regret. "Remember. You said you wouldn't ask again. And honestly, there is no point in asking, not unless you're ready to believe the answer when you hear it."

He just looked at her. She was right, and he knew

it. There was no point in her telling him the same thing again.

He closed his eyes, nodded. That soft hand slid away.

Grasping her shoulders, he set her body back from his. "Go on to your room now," he said, his voice thick with the hunger that wasn't going to be satisfied. "I'll stay with Lena awhile."

Josie showered and put on the big red T-shirt she liked to sleep in. Then she spent an hour or so at her computer, answering e-mails and checking out the Web sites of a few colleges that offered correspondence degrees. She planned to sign up for at least a course or two in the fall.

About ten-thirty, she shut the computer down and reached for the mystery that waited in the corner of her desk. When she finally closed the book, it was six minutes short of midnight. She switched off the lamp.

And then she just sat there in the dark, looking out over the moonlit garden, idly rubbing the pads of two fingers over her lips, remembering the feel of Flynt's mouth there.

Was she getting anywhere with him, really?

It was so hard to tell. And it had only been one day, after all. One day. And one night.

He'd already kissed her.

That was a good sign, wasn't it?

Then again, to be totally truthful about what had

happened, well, she'd pretty much thrown herself at him. Just pushed herself right into his arms and shoved her mouth up under his.

He'd taken it from there.

Oh, my goodness, had he ever. The only thing wrong with that kiss had been the length of it: much too short.

Josie leaned back in her desk chair and stretched. Lena usually woke around two or so. If Josie went to bed right now she could get a couple of hours' sleep before—

Josie blinked and stood from the chair. She leaned on the desk and craned close to the window.

She could have sworn...

Yes. There was someone down there—two people. A man leading a woman along the garden path. They paused. For a moment, the two shadows merged into one. Josie sighed. A kiss, a passionate one.

And also brief. Now the man was stepping back, grabbing the woman's hand again, leading her away.

The woman seemed to hesitate. The man turned back, said something, and a shaft of moonlight fell across his face.

Matt. Flynt's younger brother.

Josie smiled. How sweet. Matt and his special lady. A secret meeting in the garden in the middle of the night. Matt urged the woman onward, deeper into the shadows of the greenery. Josie, her romantic heart beating a little faster for them, leaned right up to the glass, not even pausing to think that, should one of the lovers look toward the window, her own face might very well be seen, floating ghostlike, just beyond the glass.

The woman paused again briefly and slanted a nervous look over her shoulder, the moon lighting her face as it had that of her lover. Something must have drawn her eye upward, for all at once, she was looking straight at Josie's window. For one split second, the woman's eyes locked with Josie's. Josie gasped as recognition dawned.

Then Matt pulled his lady into the shadows, and the two disappeared around a bend in the path.

Josie remembered to breathe. She sank into her chair again and stared at her dark computer screen, shaking her head in disbelief.

The woman Matt had kissed in the garden worked at the Mission Creek Library. She and Josie often exchanged how-are-you's when Josie dropped in to pick out another big stack of books.

Her given name was Rose.

And her last name was Wainwright.

Josie might have told Flynt what she'd seen in the garden in the middle of the night.

But after the toe-curling kiss in the baby's room, he decided to avoid her for two days running. By then, it was Friday. At 6:00 p.m., Grace relieved her for her weekend off.

That gave her time to think the situation over.

Really, she couldn't predict how he might react if she told him she'd seen his brother kissing a Wainwright. As a Carson, Flynt would be way too likely to mess everything up for the lovers.

Josie didn't want that. She felt kind of... What was the word? Proprietary. Yes. She felt proprietary and protective toward Matt and Rose. She knew their secret. But no one was getting it out of her. They were bucking generations of senseless hatred and bad blood and Josie was one hundred percent on their side. The way she saw it, if a Carson and a Wainwright had found love together, well, more power to them.

Flynt said things would never change. To him, Carsons and Wainwrights would forever be enemies— and he had blown his chance at love and happiness and did not deserve another.

Josie thought otherwise. To her mind, a person *had* to think otherwise. If change wasn't possible, why not give it all up now? There'd be no point in going on.

By the first Sunday in June, four days after the kiss and three days into Flynt finding an excuse to leave any room Josie happened to be in, she decided she'd had about enough of his running away from her.

She returned from her mother's house at six that evening. She had a pretty good idea he'd be stopping in to see the baby at some point. He'd probably do

what he'd done Thursday night—wait until Josie left
the nursery before going in. So she tricked him. She
put Lena to bed and she turned off the light and sat
there in the rocker in the dark, facing the door.

It took him an hour, but he came at last, hesitating
in the doorway, as if he sensed a trap. The hall light
behind him outlined his tall body, leaving the front in
shadow so she couldn't see his face.

But he saw her. "Damn it, Josie."

She stood. "I've been waiting for you."

He swore again.

She went to him in the doorway and looked up into
his shadowed face. "I want to talk to you."

"It's not a good idea." He started to turn.

She caught his hand. "Wait."

He froze.

Josie twined her fingers with his. He allowed her
to do that—not that he gave her a reassuring squeeze
or anything, but he didn't yank away. She would
think of that as a good sign.

"Please," she whispered. "Let me say what I have
to say."

She could feel his eyes on her, studying her. Finally
he agreed. "All right."

"Come on." She slid around him, keeping hold of
his hand. "Let's go where we won't wake the baby."
She tugged him toward the double doors of the sitting
room across the hall.

* * *

Should he have let her drag him into the other room? Probably not. But Flynt found himself going where she led him, anyway.

Once she got him there, she let go of his hand. He moved toward the sofa and she paused at the doors to make certain they were both firmly shut.

Flynt switched on a floor lamp at the end of the sofa, then turned as Josie came toward him. God, she was beautiful. She wore flared jeans that hugged her hips and a snug little shirt with cap sleeves. The lamplight gleamed off her pale, straight hair. Those green eyes were focused on his face and the look in them was way too knowing. She kept coming, until she was right next to him and he caught the tempting scent of her.

He gestured at the sofa beside them, waited until she sat down and then moved away and took one of the two velvet wing chairs on the other side of the big coffee table.

They regarded each other. He was frowning, but a soft smile curved that mouth of hers. Her eyes gently reproached him for his little trick of luring her to the couch—and then not staying there to sit beside her.

She stated the obvious. "The past few days you've been avoiding me."

He answered with caution. "It seemed like the best way to handle things."

"Why?"

He felt his frown deepen to a scowl. *Why?* was her

favorite question lately. She seemed to ask it every chance she got.

He was tired of responding to it. Especially since she never accepted the answers he gave her, anyway.

She must have seen that he intended to stonewall on that one. She spoke again. "You're planning to ask me to marry you, right? As soon as you get the paternity test results."

He almost blinked. But not quite. "Got it all figured out, huh?"

"Pretty much. Right now you're denying yourself. And me. I guess it makes you feel noble to do that, right?" He saw no need to reply. So he didn't. She went right on, anyway. "Well, I don't see any real point in your staying away from me. Especially if you're thinking that we're going to get married soon. It makes no sense. It's just plain dumb."

"Thanks for your input. Is that it?"

"No."

"What else, then?"

"I think it's pretty obvious. I want you to stop avoiding me." Now *she* was frowning, leaning forward across the coffee table.

He found himself thinking back on what she'd said a minute ago. About them getting married as soon as the test results came through. He realized this could be progress they were making here. "Just a minute. Is this your roundabout way of telling me that you're Lena's—"

She was shaking her head. "Don't even say it. You know what we agreed."

He told himself to ignore his own disappointment. She was right. They did have an understanding and he ought to abide by it. "Fine."

She said, "I just think, well, I hate to see us waste this time. Time is precious, Flynt. Most people don't realize how precious until most of it is gone." She had a pair of canvas sneakers on her feet, the kind with thick soles and round toes. Right then she leaned her elbows on her knees and stared down at those sneakers, as if the answer to some important question might have been scrawled across the tops of them.

He looked at those pretty, slim hands, folded between her knees, at the crown of her white-gold head, at the soft curve of her cheek. The desire to reach across the table and lay his palm against that cheek was so powerful right then, he almost gave in to it.

But she lifted her head just in time. "Maybe I shouldn't have got in your face like that the other night."

He didn't quite follow. "Got in my face?"

"You know, trapped you up against the baby's crib, practically forced you to kiss me."

That did amuse him. A low rumble of a laugh escaped him.

"Don't laugh at me." She pulled her shoulders back and stuck her chin in the air. "Please."

"Laughing? Who's laughing?"

"Oh, very funny." She stood—and then couldn't seem to decide where to go from there, so she dropped onto the couch again. "I know you think you're some big macho guy, that there is no way I could force you to kiss me. And you're right. There isn't. But I do know how you feel about me. It's the same way I feel about you. It's pretty powerful."

He opened his mouth to argue that point. And then he shut it without saying a word. Why deny what they both knew to be achingly true? He wanted her. She wanted him. It wasn't news to either of them.

She went on, "I understand, I truly do, that you don't want to give in to how you feel about me right now. And I ought to respect that. I want you to know that I *will* respect that, from now on."

He wanted to kiss her so bad, it hurt. "You will?"

She nodded. "I just want us to have a little time, you know? To talk. To laugh together. To enjoy each other's company. If you think about it, we've never done that. I've been your housekeeper and for one night, I was your lover. Now I'm Lena's nanny. And that could be a good thing."

"I never said it wasn't."

"I mean, we could use this time, if we were smart. I'm right here, in your private wing of this house— for a little while, anyway. If you'd only stop treating me like I've got some scary contagious disease, we could start getting to know each other better."

He had to admit she had a point.

She was right about something else, too. He did intend to marry her—as soon as she could bring herself to admit the truth about Lena.

He cleared his throat. "Well," he said.

"Yeah?" She leaned even closer, so damned adorably eager.

"I don't see anything wrong with what you're suggesting."

Her face seemed to glow from within. "You don't?"

"No. It makes sense to me."

She sat up straight again. "Well, good—no, better than good. Great." She stuck out her hand.

He realized she wanted him to shake on it.

Why not?

He reached across the coffee table and took her hand in his.

Nine

After their talk in the sitting room on Sunday night, Flynt stopped avoiding Josie. He came to the baby's room twice the next day. They did just what she had asked for. They talked. They played with Lena.

Monday night they had dinner together while Lena napped. Flynt had a table set up in the sitting room. They had prime Carson beef, new potatoes and asparagus.

He found he thoroughly enjoyed Josie's company. He'd always known she was bright, but he'd never realized what a pleasure it could be just to sit and talk with her. She asked incisive questions and she had her own opinions, which she rarely hesitated to share.

He enjoyed that meal so much, he suggested they do the same thing on Tuesday night.

Josie smiled at the invitation. "Flynt Carson, I was starting to think you were never going to ask."

So in the next few days, it became something of a standing date. He'd have the table set in the sitting room and they would eat dinner there together.

On Thursday he dropped in around lunchtime to find Josie in her own room, with Lena bobbing happily in a baby swing a few feet from where Josie sat at her computer, typing away.

Flynt stood in her open doorway, appreciating the view. She had that silvery hair pulled back and anchored low on her neck with one of those scrunchy things and she wore a cheerful-looking pink-and-yellow checked shirt, with a collar but no sleeves. He admired the straight, graceful line of her slim shoulders. No slouching for Josie Lavender. Even sitting at her computer, she held herself up tall and proud.

Eventually she turned to check on the baby and caught sight of him out of the corner of her eye. "Flynt." Her smile was blinding, a joy to behold. "Just a minute." She turned back to the computer and swiftly shut something down.

She hadn't exactly invited him in, but the door was open. "What's going on in here?" He crossed the small room until he stood right behind her.

In her swing, Lena made a giggling sound, then let out a big sigh. Flynt grinned at the sweet little noises, but he didn't turn. His eyes were on Josie.

Her chair had a swivel base. With a jittery trill of laughter, she slid around to face him. Her cheeks were bright pink.

Something was up. "You're nervous. What about?"

He watched her consider telling some kind of fib and then reject that idea. She let out a playful groan. "Oh, all right. I was writing in my journal. Private stuff."

He lifted an eyebrow at her. "Stuff about me?"

"You'll never know."

"Never?" He put on a wounded look.

"Well…" She relented a little. "Maybe someday. And don't worry. It's mostly good stuff. At least for the last few days it's been good stuff."

"The last few days, huh? That's not much."

"It's a start—and I mean it. My journal is private and I don't want you snooping around in it. I know you could get through my password protection in ten seconds flat. But you're an honorable man and you won't."

She was right on both counts. He was something of a whiz kid when it came to computers. He knew several computer languages. In fact, in the military, computers had been his area of expertise. He could write code and he could get through some pretty sophisticated security setups when he needed to.

But he'd never use his hacking skills to invade Josie's privacy. He put up a hand, palm out. "Your journal is safe from me."

She gave him a tender look. "I know it is."

He could have kissed her. But that wasn't allowed. And since just looking at her mouth was too much of a temptation, he looked elsewhere—at her computer screen. It was crammed full of shortcuts. "Your desktop's got way too much junk on it. You ought to clean it up. You've got icons on here you probably never use." He reached for the mouse.

She tapped his hand. "Uh-uh. Back off. This is my machine and I like it just the way it is."

"But you could—"

"No, Flynt. Leave it alone."

He shrugged. "Hey, it's your mess."

"You are so right."

"How do you like your cable modem?"

"It's great. Thanks." She moved in her chair—just enough to signal him that she wanted to get up. It wouldn't do, after all, for her to brush against him in passing if she could avoid it.

He stepped back, thinking that this was the one uncomfortable aspect of this new push to get to know each other better. They were both constantly on guard not to get too close in the physical sense, not to create any dangerous opportunities for the attraction between them to take control.

She rose to her feet and slid around him. He breathed deeply as she went by. Yeah, he was keeping hands off, but no one said he couldn't enjoy the clean scent of her hair and the subtle, womanly fragrance of her skin.

"Come on, darlin', let's get you out of there." She lifted Lena from the swing.

Flynt suggested, "How about if I have lunch sent up?"

She had the baby on her shoulder, their heads close together, dark against light. "Sandwiches? In the baby's room?"

He took it even further. "We could have a picnic, spread a blanket on the floor."

"Flynt." She gave him another one of those incredible, blinding smiles. "That's a downright whimsical idea."

"Yeah. I've always been real big on whimsy."

She kissed Lena's cheek. "How come I never noticed?"

"Well, all right," he confessed, "maybe I'm not the most whimsical guy on the planet. And even if I was, in the time we've known each other, opportunities for whimsy have often been limited."

She kissed Lena again. "Mmm. Limited. I guess that's right."

They both grew serious then, looking into each other's eyes. He was thinking of his rotten marriage, of the accident, of his battle with the bottle. He had a strong suspicion her mind was tracking along the same lines—maybe with a few extra wrinkles all her own: her mother's illness, her father's cruelty, the sad, ugly way Rutger Lavender had died. And what about Lena? That must have been damn tough for her, giving birth to their baby all on her own.

She smoothed the baby's soft dark hair. "A picnic is a great idea. Let's do it."

Flynt called downstairs and told Anita what he wanted for their picnic. A half an hour later, a maid appeared with a picnic basket and a big blanket. Flynt spread the blanket on the floor and they laid Lena in a corner of it, with her play station over her to keep her amused.

Josie loaded up a plate for him and passed him a tall glass of cold tea. "You want some honey on that biscuit?" She held up a squeeze bottle.

"Squirt it right on there."

"Don't you want it in halves first?"

He had his plate in one hand and his glass of tea in the other. He held out the plate. "Split it for me, will you?"

She picked up his biscuit and separated the two soft, warm halves. Steam spiraled up from them. "Mmm. Smells so good. Reynaldo sure knows his way around a batch of biscuits."

Reynaldo Cruz had cooked for the Carsons for over twenty years. He could be temperamental, but no one ever complained about the meals that came out of his kitchen.

Josie aimed the squeeze bottle at one biscuit half and then the other, trailing the honey in matching spirals. "How's that?" She looked up from his plate and into his eyes.

And, all at once, the whole thing was sexual.

Something tightened down inside him. Heat began to spread. All he wanted to do was lean toward her and capture that incredible mouth of hers, to share a long, slow, wet kiss. To set aside his plate and his glass of cold tea and take that squeeze bottle away from her—but maybe keep it close by. Yeah. Definite potential in a squeeze bottle of honey.

In his mind's eye, he could see it. A gleaming trail of honey dripping down onto her naked belly, filling the tiny bowl of her navel, puddling in the slight hollow beneath her rib cage, spilling over, sliding along the velvet slopes on either side of her waist. And also slowly edging into the silvery curls that covered the secret place where her thighs joined....

Josie had tipped the honey bottle upright, but stopped there. She still held it, poised above his plate. The world seemed to have spun to a halt. Her mouth had gone softer than ever. Her pupils were bigger, dark and open. To him.

"Oh, Flynt..." In a rush, she let out the breath she'd been holding.

He stared at her mouth and he accepted the fact that it was no damn good trying to keep his hands off her. He wanted a kiss and he wanted it now. He heard himself whisper, "Oh, yeah."

They leaned toward each other, a pair of magnets with complementary charges.

"Josie, I wonder if— Oh!"

The words—and the shocked exclamation at the end of them—came from the doorway in that split second before Flynt could take Josie's mouth. Josie let out a tiny cry of distress and jerked back to her side of the blanket.

Flynt sucked in a big breath and let it out with care. Then he faced the intruder. "What can we do for you, Ma?"

Grace looked as if she'd just seen the ghost of Lou Lou Wainwright, pale and Ophelia-like, skin sickly gray, lips blue, dripping water from her own drowning across the floor. "I…well, I…" Grace swallowed, put her hand against her throat.

Flynt winced at his mother's reaction. He supposed it didn't surprise him. She hadn't been given the whole story here—and she wouldn't be getting it. Not for a while. Hell, he doubted he would ever tell her all of it.

Carefully he set down his plate and glass and stood. "Ma—"

Grace put out a hand and spoke sharply. "No. Please don't say anything."

Dropping the subject suited Flynt just fine, though he had a serious suspicion he'd get an earful later, after his mother had a chance to stew on it a little. In Grace Carson's world, a man—especially a man she herself had raised up to do right—didn't make passes at the household help.

Grace put on a tight smile. "I came up to ask Josie if she would mind taking her time off a little early today. Cara has an appointment in town and my hairdresser has said she can see me at four-thirty. If Josie could go now and get back by four..."

Josie stood and brushed the biscuit crumbs from her lap. "Sure. Give me ten minutes. I'll be ready to go."

"Good, then. Ten minutes. I'll be here." Grace turned and disappeared down the hall.

Flynt and Josie were left alone with the baby, who giggled and cooed to herself on the floor while the two adults stared at each other, neither sure what to say. There was, after all, not only Grace's reaction to their changing relationship to deal with. Beyond that, they had to face the fact that if Grace hadn't walked in on them, they would have ended up in each other's arms again—which, for the time being anyway, was the one place they'd agreed not to go.

Josie worried her full lower lip for a moment. Then she dropped to a crouch on the blanket.

Flynt realized she intended to clean up the picnic they'd never had a chance to enjoy. "Leave it. One of the maids will get it."

"But—"

"Josie, leave it." His voice was gruffer than he intended it to be.

She stood again. "Well, then I guess I should—"

"Go ahead. Get your purse or whatever. Get ready to go."

But she just stood there, looking at him, worrying her lip some more.

"What?" he demanded after they'd stared at each other for several grim seconds. "Say it, whatever it is."

"It's only…"

"Yeah?"

"She was…" Josie hesitated, and then finished lamely, "…really shocked."

He wondered what she'd started out to say. "She'll get over it."

"She doesn't like the idea of you and me together. You saw that look on her face, didn't you? She doesn't like it one bit."

"She'll be fine—and I wish you'd just tell me whatever it is you're not saying."

"Oh, Flynt…"

"Just tell me."

"Well, she—she spoke to me about it."

He didn't like the sound of that. "What do you mean?"

That poor lip of hers got a little more abuse. Then she shook her head. "We'd better just talk about it later." She started to turn away. He caught her before she could escape. She looked down at where he gripped the smooth flesh of her arm, then into his eyes again. Heat seemed to arc in the air between them.

He let go. "Answer me."

She wrinkled up her nose at him. "Oh, don't get that look."

"You brought it up. Explain yourself."

Down on the blanket, Lena was starting to fuss. Josie said, "You mind if I see to the baby?"

He shrugged.

She bent, moved the play station and gathered Lena into her arms. The baby quieted instantly. "It was last week. My first day of work." Josie rocked back on her heels and stood again. "It was all real polite, what she said. And it was nothing direct." Josie turned for the changing bureau. She laid the baby down and got to work on a diaper change.

Flynt came and stood behind her—but not too close behind. "What did she say?"

"She said she thought a nanny job would be too hard on me." Josie's hands moved with smooth efficiency as she spoke. She got rid of the soiled diaper, made use of a couple of baby wipes. "She said that a woman my age should have boyfriends, an active social life. That I'd be unhappy alone with just Lena all day long."

"And that's all?"

Josie used another baby wipe on her own hands, then got down a fresh diaper and slid it under the baby. Lena giggled and waved her arms. Josie bent close to her, kissed the tiny fists as they moved in the air.

"What else?" Flynt prompted.

She smoothed the diaper in place and pressed the tabs. "I told you, it was all kind of vague. The message I got from her was that she had realized there was something going on between us. She didn't like it. So she tried to talk me out of taking care of Lena, to make sure I wouldn't be right where I am now, living in your wing of the house, around you all the time." Josie lifted the baby again.

"Here. I'll take her."

Josie handed her over. "Your mama's no fool, Flynt. She knows that you don't put a lighted match to kindling unless you plan on startin' a fire."

Flynt cradled Lena close, cupping the back of her head, damned irritated with his mother—and more than a little put out with Josie, as well. "Why didn't you tell me this before?"

She drew her shoulders back, the way she always did when she felt challenged. "I am not someone who carries tales to a man about something his mother has done. And I told you, she never said a thing I could put my finger on, anyway. I was reading between the lines."

"You should have told me."

"Well, I am telling you now." Those proud shoulders drooped a little. Lena giggled and then cooed, the sounds soft and sweet, right next to his ear. Josie stared up at him, eyes wide with apprehension. "And I'll tell you something else. You'll be hearing more about what your mother thinks of what's going on between the two of us. And it won't be vague or polite."

What could he say to that? He knew she was right.

She gave a sad little shrug. "I'd better get ready to go."

She left him standing there, holding the baby—and hoping that maybe his mother would have sense enough to think twice before butting in to a situation she didn't understand and had no business meddling in, anyway.

That night his father asked for a word with him in the downstairs study.

Ten

Ford stood from behind his massive cherrywood desk—a desk that Carson patriarchs had been sitting at since the days when Big Bill rolled his wheelchair up to it. "Cigar, son?" Ford flipped open the humidor that waited on the desk's outer edge.

Flynt dropped into a studded leather wing chair facing his father. "You know Ma would have a fit if you actually smoked one of those things."

Ford shook his white head in deepest regret and shut the cigars back up in their climate-controlled case. "'Fraid you're right. I'm not allowed any damn fun anymore." Since Ford's heart surgery, Grace watched his diet, carefully monitored his alcohol intake and strictly forbade his use of anything that involved tobacco products. Ford kept the cigars on his desk now for show and so he could hand them out to guests. He was, after all, a Carson born and raised. He had a cattleman's image to uphold and that image included being able to offer a good smoke when the occasion demanded.

Flynt asked, "What did you want to talk to me about, Dad?" As if he didn't damn well know.

Ford cleared his throat—a thoughtful kind of sound. He sat again, settling back in his huge high-backed oxblood-red leather swivel chair.

Flynt waited. Sometimes his father took a while to work himself around to the point. There was no sense in trying to hurry him up. He'd get there when he got there.

Ford leaned back farther, rested his elbows on the padded chair arms and pondered the brass chandelier overhead. Flynt waited. Eventually Ford shifted in the chair, sitting forward, resting both forearms on the desk pad and folding his beefy hands together. "Son, you've got your mother pretty worried."

Flynt said nothing. There was nothing to say, really, other than Oh? or I have? or Why is that?—all questions that would ultimately have no effect at all on the lecture his father was gearing up to deliver.

"She saw you with Josie Lavender today." Ford had scrunched his heavy eyebrows together, giving him a look both grave and reproachful. "Your mother is certain she interrupted what would have been a passionate kiss."

Again Flynt said nothing.

Ford indulged in a second throat-clearing cough. "All right. First, I suppose, I need to just ask you. How far has it gone?"

Flynt let a moment of weighted silence elapse before answering, "That's none of your business, Dad."

"Of course, it's my business. You're my son. This is my house."

Flynt couldn't let that last pass. "Hold on, Dad. I thought we'd settled all that about the house years ago. The way I remember it, we agreed that my wing of the house is *my* house, not yours. If you've decided to change the rules on me, there's no problem. I'll find someplace else to—"

"Now, now. Let's not go saying things we don't mean."

"Trust me, Dad. I mean what I'm saying. Either my wing is my own, or it's not. And if it's not, I'll move out."

"Now listen here. No one wants you moving out. It's just that your mother's been concerned about Josie Lavender ever since you insisted on hiring her."

"Why?"

"You know damn well why."

"Josie's great with Lena. She works hard. She's also dependable. I know I can count on her."

"Last year, she—"

"Forget last year. She's working out fine now and that's what matters."

Ford's eyebrows scrunched up tighter. "Look. Let's stop circling the subject here. Just be straight with me. Are you having an affair with that girl?"

That question, Flynt could answer. "No."

Ford leaned closer across the desk and pitched his voice low. "But you're headed there. Right?" He barreled on, not even pausing to wait for an answer. "What you're doing is wrong, and you know it. We've brought you up better, your mother and I. In this house, we don't take advantage of the help. Josie Lavender is a beautiful and sweet girl, I know she is. But I also know damn well you don't have marriage on your mind. And since marriage is out, all that's left is a love affair. And that's not fair to Josie. She hasn't had it easy in her life, and you know it. She seems to me to be someone who is only trying to live her life with some degree of dignity. And you have to remember your position in this community. You have no right to go taking advantage of those less fortunate than you are."

"I'm not taking advantage of anyone." And he wasn't. Not currently, anyway. Last year was another story. But Ford didn't even know about last year.

"I beg to differ, son. She is the nanny and you are the boss. You're the one with the power and she depends on you for her living. And there's no question of marriage, under any circumstances. That, to me, is taking advantage."

Flynt decided he might as well go ahead and state his intention. "Dad, you've got it wrong. Chances are, I will marry Josie."

Ford sat up ramrod-straight. "You'll *what?*"

"If things...work out between us, I'm going to make Josie my wife."

"You can't mean that."

"I can and I do."

"Son…" Ford sat back in the chair again. Now he looked infinitely sad. "I understand. I do. You have no idea how well. Once, years ago—before I ever met your mother—there was someone else. I would have married her, but circumstances intervened. And I'm grateful every day of my life that they did. Your mother was the woman for me. Born to a good family, well brought-up, kind-hearted and smart, not to mention so beautiful she still takes my breath away."

"Dad—"

"No. Wait. Let me finish, now. I'm trying to tell you that your mother is just exactly the woman I needed at my side. And every day of my life I'm grateful I didn't blow my chance with her before she even came along. There'll be someone for you, too. You'll see. An equal. Someone who will fit in with your family. Someone who will know how to handle herself in the circles you travel in."

Flynt couldn't take it anymore. "Someone like Monica, you mean."

Ford did some sputtering. "Well now, son, you and I both know that Monica—"

"She was a Waverly of the damn Atlanta Waverlys. She fit in around here and she fit in big time. She was everything you and Ma ever dreamed you might get in a daughter-in-law. And my marriage to her was a complete disaster."

"Monica was…high-strung."

"I'm not blaming Monica."

"Well, now, neither am I."

"I'm saying that the marriage was no good. And Monica's 'fitting in' and having 'the right upbringing' and being born to 'a good family' didn't matter one damn bit. We wanted different things and we made each other miserable."

"Yes. And you're still confused by all that, by what happened with Monica. Your mother and I would hate to see you make a wrong choice on the rebound. There has to be some…common ground, in a marriage. There has to be shared experience and similar expectations of life. The two should have an understanding of each other's—"

Flynt had heard all he intended to hear. He stood. "Dad, what you're really trying to tell me here is that Josie isn't good enough to marry a Carson. And I'm telling you that she damn well is good enough. More than good enough. If there's anyone *not* good enough in this match, I'm it."

Ford shook his head. "You're too hard on yourself. You've always been that way. I know a lot of things didn't work out the way you think they should have. But that doesn't mean you have to compound the problem by hooking up with a woman who is completely unsuited to you."

Flynt felt his temper rising. He ordered it down. "Have a little respect, Dad. Give a man the right to make his own decisions about who's suited to him and who's not.''

''You're making a big mistake.''

''I'm doing what I think is best.''

Ford's tanned, lined face had a mournful cast now. ''You have that look, son, that look that tells me you've made up your mind and there'll be no changing it.''

''You've got it right, Dad. Chances are, I'll marry Josie Lavender. You and Ma had better start getting used to the idea.''

''Marriage...'' Ford ran one of those beefy hands down the front of his face. Then he sat up straight again, eyes narrowing as awareness dawned. ''Wait a minute.''

Flynt's gut tightened. ''What?''

''The baby...''

Flynt kept his face absolutely blank.

But Ford was catching on, anyway. ''It's the baby, isn't it? This has to do with little Lena, doesn't it? Tell me now. You want a mother for that baby and you've settled on Josie.''

Flynt gave his father only silence.

''My God.'' Judging by his slack-jawed expression, Ford had put a little more of it together. ''Flynt Carson, is Josie Lavender that baby's mother?''

Flynt pointedly refused to answer.

Ford let out a heavy sigh. ''You're not going to tell me, are you?''

"No, Dad. I'm sorry. Looks like you'll just have to let me live my own damn life."

"But she *could* be the mother, right? And that's why the poor girl left out of nowhere last year. Because you took advantage of her and then either sent her away or she ran off on her own."

Ford had hit the nail on the head and driven it straight home. But Flynt only stared at him, admitting nothing.

Ford let out a low growl. "What in hell is going on around here?"

"I've said all I can say for right now."

"You've said exactly nothing."

"Sorry, it's the best I can do."

Flynt went straight to his own wing of the house. He found Josie sitting in the rocker in the baby's room, rocking Lena off to sleep.

She'd run up the shades and turned off the lamps. The soft glow of moonlight and the slight spill of brightness from the hall sconces provided the only light. Still, he could see them both clearly enough in the silvery dimness.

Josie saw him, too. She put a finger to her lips in a signal for silence. He nodded and entered the shadowy space, then waited as she rose from the rocker and carried the baby over to the crib. She laid Lena down and then remained there, hovering over her, looking down, moonlight slanting across her hair and cheek, making them gleam, her hair like spun silver, her cheek like the petal of a white, white rose.

Finally she straightened.

"Asleep?" he whispered.

"Mmm-hmm."

He held out his hand. She looked at it, suspicious and yet eager, too. He knew exactly how she felt.

"Let's go where we can talk."

Slowly she reached out and laid her hand in his.

He led her to the sitting room and pulled her down onto the sofa.

She looked in his eyes. "What happened?"

Was there any point in telling her the things that his father had said? If there was, he couldn't see it.

He knew his parents. If he married this woman, they'd accept it. Eventually. They might have their own somewhat snobbish ideas about what sort of woman he should hook up with, but both Ford and Grace Carson were fair people at heart. Besides, Josie already knew how Grace felt about the two of them. No need to beat a dead horse.

The point now, as Flynt saw it, was to make it clear to everyone that he wasn't sneaking around with Josie. He was proud to stand beside her. This was no backstairs romance—or at least, it wasn't anymore. When the truth came out about Lena, they would have to present a united front. Might as well get started on that.

"I want you to go out with me," he told her. "Tomorrow night. We'll go to the club, to the Empire Room."

Her wide eyes got wider. "The Empire Room." She gently pulled her hand from his. "Oh, Flynt, I don't know. The Empire room is so...formal."

"You're right about that." He privately considered the Empire Room overrated. The food wasn't as good as it should be; Harvey claimed to be working on that. And the décor was a little too luxurious, almost oppressively so. It was all pale blues and ivories accented with an excess of gold leaf—on the chairs, in the chandeliers, even on the ornate medallions that decorated the blue watered-silk walls. In the Empire Room, a coat and tie were required, and the ladies always dressed their best.

Josie suggested hopefully, "Maybe we could go somewhere a little more comfortable."

"No," he said. "We couldn't."

The corners of her mouth flattened out. "Well, why not? I'd have a lot better time someplace we could relax a little, be easy with each other."

He caught her hand again, captured it completely in both of his. "You said you wanted a chance for us."

A sweet flush traveled up her smooth throat. "Oh, Flynt. I do."

"Well, this is part of it, Josie. You and me together. And not somewhere private, not somewhere cozy or intimate, not right now. No. It's got to be out in the open, someplace where people go to see and be seen."

She pulled back a little, though not far, as he refused to let go of her hand. "We're making some kind of big statement here, is that it?"

"What's wrong with that? It's time people started seeing us out together."

She was frowning. "What happened? Something happened, didn't it? Did Grace—"

"Don't worry about Grace. She's hardly said two words to me since this afternoon."

"She's not speaking to you? Oh, Flynt."

"I didn't say that."

"But if she—"

"Josie, listen. She's speaking to me. Stop worrying about her." He lifted her hand, kissed the back of it, slanted her a tender look.

That pretty flush moved up over her cheeks. But she was no fool and she wouldn't completely let go of her suspicions. "Something is going on here."

"That's right. I'm asking you out. To the Empire Room. And you keep refusing to say you'll go with me."

"But—"

"No more buts. Just say yes or no."

"Flynt, I—"

"Josie, yes or no?"

"Oh, all right."

"Damn. Was that a yes? Finally?"

"Very funny. You know, I've heard the food's not very good at the Empire Room."

He put on a scowl. "Who told you that?"

"Oh, please. If I tell you who told me, some head somewhere would probably roll."

"You have an inflated idea of my influence."

"No, I do not and— Wait a minute. Who's going to watch Lena?"

"That's not your problem. You're off for the weekend anyway at six, aren't you?"

"Yes. And I'm going to need a few hours before that, too."

"Because?"

The look she gave him then was infinitely superior. "Fashion emergency."

"What?"

"Flynt Carson, when a girl gets invited to the Empire Room and there are not even twenty-four hours between the invitation and the date—that is called a fashion emergency."

"You mean you want to buy a new dress."

"You are such a smart man."

Eleven

Flynt was to pick Josie up at Alva's at eight. Cara relieved her at three the next afternoon.

"Big date, huh?" Cara was grinning.

"You heard?"

"I did. I think it's great—you and my big brother."

"Too bad your mother doesn't feel the same way."

"Just wait."

"For what?"

"For her to realize he could be happy with you. That'll change her attitude. And it's not going to take that long, either."

"You seem pretty certain."

"Well, I do know my own mother. She's got her faults, but she's not blind. Pretty soon, she'll have to notice that Flynt has actually started smiling again now and then."

"Oh, I hope so."

"Don't worry. It will work out. Now, I heard you're going shopping."

"I need a great dress and I need it now."

"Try Mission Creek Creations."

Josie tried not to wince. Mission Creek Creations

was the town's most exclusive dress shop. All the debs went there to have their fancy white dresses made to order for the annual Lone Star County Debutante Ball. It was also the place where brides from the best families found their beautiful, extravagant gowns, where professional women could get designer-label business clothes, not to mention a wide range of gorgeous, glittery things suitable for after-five. Josie probably could find exactly what she wanted in a place like that. Too bad it was way out of her price range.

Cara laughed. "Check the sale racks in back, on the ready-to-wear side. You'd be surprised the kind of bargains you can find."

Though time was running short and she knew she ought to head for that nice, middle-of-the-road department store in the new mall out on Mission Creek Road, Josie threw good sense to the wind and took Cara's advice.

The shop was charming and very feminine, all in pink and white and gold—everything but the beautiful dresses, which came in a whole rainbow of colors. Josie longed to linger at each rack she passed. But one glance at the price tag dangling from a shimmering sleeve fixed that.

She strode purposefully to the back, where two big round racks had pretty pink signs propped up above them, each printed with Sale in flowing gold script. She found her size and checked a few tags first.

Still very pricey.

But this was a big occasion and she wanted to look her best.

After a cursory glance at the first rack, she went on to the second one and started sliding the dresses around, looking for *the* dress, the one that was so perfect, so stunning, so absolutely wonderful, the giant price tag wouldn't even matter.

"This would look lovely on you." The voice, soft and well-bred and vaguely familiar, came from behind Josie, at the other rack.

Josie turned—and had to bite back a sharp cry of dismay. She knew that face, that smooth, straight hair as black as a crow's wing. Those eyes the color of a Texas bluebonnet. She gulped. "Uh, Ms. Wainwright. How are you?"

"Hello, Josie." Those violet eyes seemed a little bit worried—and, somehow, a little bit teasing, as well. "Call me Rose, please. We certainly know each other at least that well."

"Yes. All right, Rose." Josie kept picturing that embrace down in the dark garden at the Carson house, and then, right after, this woman's face tipped up toward the window, the moonlight making her pale skin glow.

"I do think this is a good color for you." Rose held out a dress—a simple scoop-necked knee-length sheath of some lovely, satiny fabric. It was a deep green in color, a green that seemed to change as light played over it, showing hints of a lighter green and gold and even black.

Josie took the dress. "Thanks. I'll try it."

Rose remarked softly, "I haven't seen you at the library in a while."

"I've been real busy. But I don't think I have any overdue books..."

"Hmm," said Rose, her face so serious, it made Josie want to smile. "Overdue books. Yes. Now you know why I followed you in here. 'A-ha,' I said to myself. 'There's that Josie Lavender. I'll just go after her right here and now, and let her know what I think of the way she's let her fines pile up.'"

The two women stared at each other, and then, out of nowhere, they were both laughing—slightly frantic laughter, on both of their parts. They put their hands across their mouths and tried to hold it in, but it threatened to overpower them, right there between the two sale racks in the back of Mission Creek Creations.

"Is everything all right here?" The plump, kind-faced shop owner came bustling up to them.

Rose quickly composed herself, and Josie struggled to do the same. Rose said, "Oh, yes, Mrs. McKenzie. We're just fine. Just looking."

"Well, good, then. How have you been, Rose?"

"I'm doing all right." Rose introduced the shop

owner and told Josie, "Mrs. McKenzie made my deb dress a few years back."

"Yes." The shop owner patted Rose's arm. "Rose is one of my girls." She touched Josie's shoulder. "I hope you're finding everything you need?"

"Oh, yes. Thanks."

"You be sure to let me know if there's anything I can do."

Rose took the green dress back from Josie and handed it to Mrs. McKenzie. "She'll be trying this one on."

"A good choice." Mrs. McKenzie nodded at Josie. "Wonderful with those eyes of yours. I'll just get a dressing room started for you, shall I?"

As soon as the shop owner turned her back on them, Rose grabbed Josie's arm and pulled her behind the second sale rack. She glanced nervously around and when she was sure no one was near, she whispered, "I didn't tell Matt that I saw you in the window, that I was sure you had seen us. He's very...protective of me. And if he knew someone had seen us, well, I can't say for sure how he'd react. I just had this absolute certainty that you wouldn't say anything."

"Oh, I didn't, Rose. I swear. The more I thought about it, the more saying anything seemed like a real bad idea. So I never said a word."

"I hope you never will."

"I won't. Not ever. I promise."

"I believe you. And I'm grateful. It's hopeless, between Matt and me. We both know it, and yet, somehow…"

"Oh, Rose. Don't. Never say that love is hopeless."

"Not even if it happens to be the truth?"

"You can't just give in to that kind of attitude. You have to fight, to make things better. It's the only way."

Rose was shaking her head. "You don't understand."

"I do."

"You think you do. But you weren't born a Wainwright—or a Carson, for that matter. My great-grandfather put Matt's in a wheelchair. And that was just the beginning." Rose sighed. "I know, I know. I can see it in your eyes. You've heard all this before. It's probably nothing much more than an old, sad story to you. But to us—to my family—it's our lives. It's what we are. We *hate* the Carsons, Josie. And they hate us. That's the way it's been for generations. I don't see any way it will ever change."

To Josie's mind, Rose sounded way too much like Flynt. *Things are the way they are,* he'd insisted a little over a week ago now. *They're not going to change.*

And yet, they were changing. Witness herself. Here at Mission Creek Creations buying a fancy dress to wear on a date with Flynt that very night.

"Oh, Rose, if you love him, you should stick with him. No matter what. No matter how impossible the two of you together might seem."

Rose's smile was so resigned, it made Josie want to cry. "Considering all you've been through in your life, Josie Lavender, you certainly are a naive little thing."

Josie ended up trying on only one dress—the one that Rose had chosen. It was just right. Simple and gorgeous, good against her skin, picking up the color in her eyes. And it fit as if it had been made for her personally.

Mrs. McKenzie *oohed* and *ahhed* over it, then insisted she slip on an incredible pair of evening sandals, black, with bits of glittery green stone embedded in the straps. "I'm having a special sale right now," Mrs. McKenzie explained. "If you buy the sandals and this beautiful little bag, you get the dress for half off the sale price you see on the tag."

That made the whole ensemble almost the same price she would have paid for the dress alone. "Some sale," said Josie, hardly believing her luck.

"Yes," said Mrs. McKenzie, a knowing gleam in her eye. "Isn't it, though?"

Flynt arrived at Alva's at eight on the nose. He was driving one of the Carson Cadillacs. Josie was so nervous, she was standing at the window peeking through the curtain, waiting to catch sight of him, when he drove up. She'd been ready for over an hour by then.

From the sofa behind her, Alva chuckled—carefully, so as not to get a wheezing fit going. "Hon, didn't anyone ever tell you it's important to make a man wait?"

"Oh, Mama, you know acting cool about things is not my style. It's him! He's just getting out of that beautiful car. Oh, he is handsome."

"All dressed up in a suit?"

"You bet he is. He's coming up the walk." She dropped the edge of the curtain, turned to her mother, smoothed her dress. "How do I look?"

"Fantastic."

"Oh, Mama. That is exactly the right thing to say."

There was a tap on the door. Josie pulled it open.

Flynt said, "Wow."

"You don't look half-bad yourself, Flynt Carson."

Flynt drove the fine car up the curving oak-lined driveway that led to the portico in front of the clubhouse at the Lone Star Country Club. An attendant stepped right up and pulled open Josie's door. He helped her out of the car and then hurried around to open Flynt's door, too. Then he took Flynt's place behind the wheel and drove the car away.

Flynt wrapped Josie's hand around his arm and led her up the steps to the entrance. The glass doors swung wide. They went through into the huge lobby tiled in Texas pink granite, past the clubhouse's famous pink granite fountain, which sent glittering cascades of water halfway to the ceiling high above.

The Empire Room was right off the lobby. And the maître d' was waiting for them. "Mr. Carson, how are you tonight?"

"Just great, Marcus."

"Wonderful." The maître d' nodded at Josie. "Welcome to the Empire Room." She gave him a smile. He took a couple of gold-tasseled menus from a rack on the reservation desk. "This way."

The minute they were seated, a short, balding fellow in a black suit with a black bow tie came scurrying up to them. Flynt introduced him as Harvey Small, the club manager.

Harvey said he was delighted to make her acquaintance. He suggested they try the veal medallions and then bustled away.

A waiter appeared to discuss the wine list. Flynt sent Josie a questioning look. She shook her head, so he said they wouldn't be having wine tonight.

People waved from other tables. A few even stopped by to say hello as the maître d' led them to tables of their own. Then Flynt would introduce Josie and there would be polite smiles and nice-to-meet-you's.

With all the folks to greet, it seemed to take forever just getting their order in. Finally they'd chosen their appetizer and their soup and even the main course—those veal medallions that Harvey Small had recommended.

When his club soda came, Flynt toasted her with it. She lifted her water goblet and clicked her glass against his.

It was going pretty well, she thought. She wasn't near as nervous as she'd expected to be. If the rich and powerful in the Empire Room thought she was some kind of upstart intruder, they all had the grace to keep their opinions to themselves, to smile and say, "Lovely to meet you, Josie," and leave it at that.

And Flynt—well, he really seemed to be having a good time. He talked to her easily, telling her tales of his buddies from VMI—the Virginia Military Institute—who had all been members of the same unit in the war in the Persian Gulf.

They were halfway through the veal medallions—which were a little tough, in Josie's opinion, though, of course, she didn't say so—when two handsome, Latin-looking fellows took a table not too far from theirs.

Flynt exchanged stiff nods with both of the men.

Josie leaned close across the table. "They are…?"

"The taller one is Ricky Mercado. The other's Frank Del Brio."

"Oh, my."

"Yeah. 'Oh, my' is right."

"Ricky Mercado was part of your unit in the war, wasn't he?"

"Yeah. We were friends at one time."

"But then..."

"Haley Mercado drowned. She was his sister, after all. Ricky blamed us—me and Spence, Tyler and Luke. And rightfully so, as I've already explained to you."

She sent him a chiding look. "Stop that."

"What?"

"Guilt-tripping. It's not allowed. Not tonight."

He grinned then. "Yes, ma'am."

She pitched her voice low, the perfect level for dishing the dirt. "I heard that Frank Del Brio was engaged to Haley right before she died."

"Yeah. None of us could believe that, really, that she'd hook up with him."

"Pressure from her father, maybe?"

"I'm pretty sure of it. Haley was beautiful and bright and she deserved better than a crook like Del Brio, as far as we were concerned."

"*We* meaning you and Spencer—"

"And Tyler and Luke. All the usual suspects. Truth is, we were all half in love with her. None of us liked Del Brio. We knew he was as crooked as they come."

"So then it's true what they say? About the Mercados and Frank Del Brio?"

He chuckled. "You mean, is there really such a thing as the Texas Mafia?"

She nodded and sipped from her water goblet. "Well, is there?"

"'Fraid so. Though if you ask any one of the Mercados, you can bet they'll tell you they made all their money in that paving and contracting business they own. From what I understand, Ricky's still more in the legit end of the business. It's Frank Del Brio who's next in line to take over as mob boss, after Carmine."

"Carmine. That's Ricky's uncle?"

"Right."

"They're all members of the country club?"

"Right again. The Mercados have been members for generations now. They conduct more of their business here than I would like. But they're very generous. The club receives major endowments from them on a regular basis. Truth is, a lot of what you see when you look around this place was paid for by Mercado money."

Josie was shocked. "Mafia money?"

"That's not what I said."

"But—"

"The money the Mercados give the club is always what you could call clean money. It comes from Mercado Brothers Paving and Contracting, or from Carmine's personal bank accounts."

"But still—"

"Josie. Your naiveté is showing."

Naive. It was the same thing Rose had called her that afternoon.

Flynt must have seen her expression change. "What's wrong?"

Of course, she couldn't say. She'd sworn she wouldn't and she meant to keep her word. "Nothing. Just…life, I guess."

"You look sad."

She picked up her napkin from her lap and patted it against her mouth. "Well, I'm not." She slanted him a playful look. "What's for dessert?"

Another waiter appeared to clear off their plates. Flynt asked to see the dessert cart. They split something sinfully chocolate, which was the best part of the meal, in Josie's opinion.

Once the dessert plates were cleared away, Flynt leaned close across the table. "See? Coming here wasn't so painful, was it?"

She only smiled at him. He was right. It hadn't been bad at all.

"Ready to go?"

"Well, I could use about five minutes to put on fresh lipstick, if that's okay?"

He told her where to find the nearest ladies' room. She picked up her small beaded bag and slid out of her gilded blue chair. She had to walk past several tables where wealthy club members sat, eating their big cuts of prime rib and their slightly tough veal. Diamonds glittered at the throats of the women, and the men wore expensive suits and watches that cost more than Josie had made in the past year.

But she didn't feel anxious. She didn't feel less than them. She knew she looked good and she carried herself well. If things worked out between her and Flynt, she could get along in this world. She was smart and she learned fast. In a few years they would think of her as one of them.

Now, if Grace Carson would only hurry up and realize that.

She went through an archway and found herself in a sort of hallway with a wall on one side masking off the luxurious dining room she'd just left. On the other side, sets of arched French doors led out onto a patio. Josie turned toward the ladies' room, which was down at one end, and right then, the door opened. A man came out. He had mussed hair, a crooked tie—and lipstick smeared across his mouth.

It was Frank Del Brio, the up-and-coming Texas mob boss.

Josie gaped. Frank Del Brio didn't miss a beat. He straightened his tie, and he raked his wild black hair back into place with splayed fingers and quickly rubbed the telltale red smudges from his mouth. He clicked his tongue in a rude way and gave Josie a wink. Then he went on by.

Josie hesitated to enter the ladies' room. What would she find on the other side of that door? Nothing too embarrassing, she hoped. She stood in the aisle for several seconds, thinking she'd give whoever was in there an opportunity to make herself presentable.

Finally, it just got too silly, lurking in that hallway, waiting for…what? She wasn't quite sure. She continued on to the door and pushed it open.

In the glass and marble confines beyond, Josie found one woman—fully dressed, thank God—standing at the mirrors. The woman was small, maybe five-two or so, with a short mop of carrot-red hair. She wore what a lot of the staff at the club wore, a black skirt and white shirt. She was freshening her lipstick, looking very cool and collected.

Too bad her skirt was only half-zipped.

She must have realized the problem, because she set the lipstick down, turned from the mirror, and gave Josie a long, slow, insolent look as she reached behind herself and did the zipper up the rest of the way.

Josie glanced down and saw the name tag pinned above her left breast: Hello, it read. I'm Erica.

When Josie met the woman's eyes again, a too-friendly smile had replaced the insolent stare. "Hi."

Josie nodded and kept walking, thinking she wouldn't like to tangle with that one. She entered the first stall. When she came out, the redhead named Erica was gone.

They were back in the Cadillac, headed toward town, when Flynt suggested, "Want to stop in at the Saddlebag for a drink?"

Josie sent him a fond look. He didn't want the evening to end any more than she did.

He lifted an eyebrow at her. "Well, I guess I should say that *you're* welcome to a drink. I'll have my usual."

"I'd love to stop at the Saddlebag for a drink."

So they went to the quiet, dim bar out on Gulf Road a few miles east of town. They took one of the tables not far from the bar itself. Flynt order his club soda and Josie had a 7-Up and he reached across the table and she put her hand in his.

It felt lovely. Absolutely right. The two of them, here in the dimness, holding hands across the scratched cocktail table, listening to Shania Twain not too loud on the jukebox and hearing the click of pool balls in the back room as somebody took somebody else at eight ball.

She told him about Frank Del Brio coming out of the ladies' room with lipstick on his mouth and his tie undone, and about the woman named Erica, too.

Flynt shook his head. "I'll talk to Harvey. I think I remember that little redhead. A waitress. Clawson, I think it is. Erica Clawson."

"Flynt, I'm not trying to get the poor woman fired."

"Don't worry. I'm not having her fired just because she and Del Brio have something going on. I'll just make a note of it to Harvey. He can keep his eyes open. And he can warn her that the hanky panky in the ladies' room is to stop as of now.''

"I do mean it, I don't want to see her lose her job…''

''But?''

''Well, I sure didn't like her much. Something real phony about her, you know? She gave me the evil eye when I first walked in on her, and then, out of nowhere, she put on this cute, sweet smile.'' Josie shivered. ''It was downright creepy.''

He was grinning at her. ''But you don't want her fired.''

''Well, now, Flynt, even a mean girl's gotta eat. Is that a slow song I hear on the jukebox?''

His hand tightened around hers. ''Dance?''

''Oh, yes.''

He stood and he took her in his arms. There wasn't much of a dance floor, really, just a wide space between the tables. But Josie didn't care and Flynt didn't seem to, either. He cradled her close and they swayed to the music.

It was heaven, just being in his arms. For so long she hadn't dared to dream he would ever hold her close again. But here they were, on a small square of floor at the Saddlebag, together, touching in all the tempting ways people could touch in a dance, a sexy, slow love song leading them on.

When the song ended, she lifted her head from his

shoulder and looked up at him. He looked down at her and there was nothing else in the world right at that moment, but her eyes meeting his eyes, the two of them in some soft, hazy place, with their arms around each other.

He lowered his mouth and captured hers and she sighed, opening to him, aroused in the deepest, truest way. She felt utterly his, and so glad of that fact.

Another slow love song started up and they were dancing again—well, kind of swaying to the music, anyway, and kissing as they swayed. Nobody in the bar seemed to care or to notice, which was another good thing about the Saddlebag. Folks tended to mind their own business there.

After a while that second song ended. Flynt pulled away enough to look into her eyes again. He whispered her name.

She heard the question in it and nodded.

He took her hand and led her out of there.

Twelve

They stopped at a convenience store on the way into town.

Flynt went in alone and came out with a brown paper bag. Josie knew what it contained. And she knew what he was thinking, that he'd see to it there was no chance she'd end up pregnant this time around.

When he got back in the car, he leaned across the console and kissed her. Then he looked at her, a probing kind of look. She waited for him to ask the question he'd promised he wouldn't ask again.

But then he only gave her a tender smile, moved back behind the wheel and started up the car.

She wanted to check on her mother. He went into the house with her and waited in the front room while she looked in on Alva.

"Sound asleep," Josie told him when she emerged from the tiny hallway that led to the bedrooms. "I'll just write her a quick note." She got a piece of paper and a pencil and wrote that she'd gone back to Carson Ranch, that she'd stop by tomorrow for an hour or two in the afternoon. She propped the note against the saltshaker on the kitchen table.

They returned to the ranch, where they found Grace asleep in the rocker in Lena's room, a novel open on her lap, a small lamp still lit beside her, her reading glasses slipping down her nose.

Flynt set the brown bag he'd brought from the convenience store on the low table by the door. Then he went to his mother, bent close to her and whispered, "Ma."

Grace started and jerked upright, her eyes popping open. "What in the—" She looked at her son. And then she looked at Josie, standing a few feet away. When her gaze moved back to Flynt, something happened in her face, a softening. "Oh," she said, as if someone had just given her some crucial piece of information and she was accepting it, acknowledging that she'd heard and understood. "Well," she said quietly. "I guess I'll go on to bed now."

"'Night, Ma."

Grace closed her book, slid her reading glasses into their case and pushed herself from the chair. She looked right at Josie. "I suppose things tend to work out, after all, don't they?"

"Yes, Mrs. Carson. If you let them, they do."

"You'll call me Grace now, won't you?"

Josie nodded. "I will."

Grace whispered another good-night and left them. Josie turned to Flynt. He was perhaps five feet away, near the chair that still rocked a little in an echo of Grace's presence there. He held out his hand.

With a small, glad cry, she went to him, reaching toward the hand that reached out to her. He caught her fingers in his, gave a tug—and she landed right where she wanted to be: in his arms.

"A kiss," he whispered into her upturned face.

"Oh, yes."

She gave him her mouth and he plundered it, tenderly, sweetly, oh, so very thoroughly.

When he drew back, he slid a hand along her arm and captured her fingers again. He turned to pull her toward the door.

Josie cast a glance at the baby's crib. "Oh, wait," she whispered.

So they tiptoed over there, together, just to make certain Lena was sleeping soundly.

She was. They stood over her, holding hands. At that moment, Josie felt such gratitude toward the dark-haired darling in that crib. Really, this child had made tonight possible.

Standing over the little angel now, Josie knew with certainty what the future would bring. She and Flynt would share a good marriage. They'd have several children. It would be all she'd ever dreamed of. Her sweetest, most impossible secret yearnings all coming true.

Yes, there would be another rough time to get through: when the results of that test came and the truth had to be faced. But they would get through it; Josie just knew they would.

Hadn't they won Grace over? Hadn't they gone out to the Lone Star Country Club together, and hadn't it worked out just fine?

And most important, wasn't Flynt slowly giving up that terrible promise he'd made to himself after Monica died? Yes. He was smiling more. He was... happier.

He was learning to live—and to love—again.

"Lena's fine," Flynt whispered.

"Yes, she is."

"Come on." He sounded urgent, hungry. She felt the same. He turned for the door, still holding tight to her hand, pausing only to grab the brown bag off the table as they went by.

His bedroom suite was as she remembered it.

He'd ordered it all done over when he got sober, a year after the accident that took Monica and their unborn child. The colors were masculine—strong, deep and rich reds and maroons, blacks and midnight-blues. The door from the hallway opened into the sitting area, with its black damask wing chairs and a sofa patterned in maroon and blue—the blue so dark it almost looked black. There were lamps with cloisonné bases and tables inlaid with jade.

Flynt pulled her in there, shut the door and turned

the latch as well as a dial beside the door. Soft recessed lights glowed overhead.

He backed her up against that door and started kissing her again. He kissed her mouth and then he trailed a string of kisses up to her temple, down along her cheek to her mouth again, where he lingered—but not for long.

Right away, his mouth went on the prowl once more. He kissed her throat with wet, sucking kisses. She moaned. He made an answering sound deep in his throat.

He dropped the brown bag. She heard it fall to the floor not far from their feet. His hands found the zipper at the back of her dress. He caught the tab and she heard that shivery, sizzling sound as it went down. She felt the air against her back. And then his hands were there, on her bare skin, caressing, driving her wonderfully crazy, so sweetly mad.

He took the sides of the dress and peeled it over her shoulders. At his urging, she slid her arms out. He took the dress down, working it over her hips until it fell to her feet—her little black panties going down with it.

When she stepped free of the fabric, he scooped up the dress and the little scrap of panties and sent them sailing toward a chair. It was a hot South Texas night, and she hadn't worn any stockings. The gorgeous sandals Mrs. McKenzie had talked her into buying looked good without them, anyway. So what she had left right then were the sandals and a black bra that matched the panties—or at least, for about ten more seconds she had a black bra.

Flynt unhooked it and tossed it atop the rest of her clothes.

Which left her standing there, naked from the ankles up.

He took her mouth again, and her knees went to jelly. She clutched his shoulders and pushed at his jacket. He took the hint and let her shove it off his shoulders, catching it as it fell and sending it flying.

He breathed her name against her skin, over and over as his lips moved on her body. His mouth closed on a hard, aching nipple. She cried out. He sucked at her, deeply, and she arched her back, heat pooling in her belly, moving outward, turning her inside out, making her ready, so ready. For him.

He drew on her breast and he slipped a hand between them, stroking her stomach, so she gasped and moaned some more. And then that hand went lower.

He touched the tight pale curls at the place where her thighs joined. Oh, she just knew she was going to melt right there, just slide down to the soft carpet underfoot, her whole body gone liquid.

His mouth slid upward again to claim hers. She kissed him. And she put her hands on his chest, set her fingers to the task of unbuttoning his shirt.

It wasn't easy, but she managed it, kissing him the whole time. She shoved that shirt off his big shoulders and then she pressed herself against him, her bare breasts to his fine, hard chest. Down below, he kept on tormenting her. His fingers moved lower still, parting her. She groaned into his mouth.

And then he broke the endless kiss they shared, pressing his forehead against hers as his hand continued, stroking fast and then slowly, a rhythm that drove her wild, that made her whole body burn.

She couldn't stay standing, couldn't hold herself upright. So she let go, just slid right down that door to the soft, thick carpet below. He went with her, bending to a crouch, then helping her, urging her to stretch out.

And to open her legs for him.

As if she could have done anything else right then.

His hand kept on, as he kissed his way downward, his tongue sliding along her throat, leaving a trail of hot wetness that the caress of the air made cool. He lingered briefly at her breasts, taking one and then the other into his mouth, swirling his tongue over the nipples, drawing so deeply that she felt as if a thread of pure desire had pulled itself taut from the place where he kissed her down into the melting hot center of her sex.

And then his mouth moved lower still. His tongue trailed over her navel, dipping in briefly, then down…and down….

He settled himself between her legs. She didn't object—why should she? His kiss, his touch—it was all that she wanted. All she'd secretly yearned for through the long months just passed.

He said her name. She opened her eyes, looked into his.

And he lowered his head and kissed her—kissed her in that most secret of places. She let out a cry, clutching for him, her fingers sliding through his silky brown hair. And she called out his name, once and then again and then again and again.

The whole world seemed to expand. There was heat and brightness behind her eyes. And then the wonderful, hot pulsing of release began.

He kept his mouth on her, until the ripples of completion faded. Then he lifted his head once more and, once again, she was looking down the length of her own naked body and into those blue, blue eyes of his.

And then she couldn't bear it, meeting his gaze right then. With a sigh, she turned away. She felt...shy at that moment. And also lazy and very naughty and extremely satisfied.

He moved, gently disentangling himself. He rolled to the side and sat, his back to her. With a long sigh, she turned her head his way again and watched as he swiftly and rather ruthlessly began stripping off the rest of his clothes.

"Flynt." She reached out, touched the tender place at the small of his back.

He sent her a hot glance over his shoulder.

She didn't have anything to say to him, really. She

just wanted the contact again, to feel his eyes meeting hers. He gave her that, then turned back to his task, yanking off his boots and socks, and slacks and briefs.

At last he was naked, too. He turned back to her, bent over her, put his mouth on hers again.

More kisses. Endless kisses. Kisses she needed to give—and to get. They had so many kisses to make up for. So many kisses missed. Almost a year's worth of kisses, really, that they should have been sharing, since the last time they'd loved.

And then he took his mouth from hers. She forced her heavy eyelids open, feeling drugged with loving, and made a questioning sound.

"I want you in my bed."

He didn't seem to require an answer, but she nodded anyway.

He grabbed the brown paper bag he'd dropped earlier and, scooping her tight against his broad chest, rose to his knees and then all the way to his full height.

He carried her to the big bed across the room and laid her down on the dark coverlet. It took him only a moment to deal with the contents of the bag.

She reached out and pulled him down into her eager arms. He entered her in one smooth thrust. She cried out, but only with pleasure, with pure happiness.

He lifted up on his elbows as he pressed more deeply into her down where their bodies were joined. "Josie," he whispered, his voice ragged with need.

"Yes. Oh, yes…"

They shared another long, intimate look, and then his mouth came down and they were kissing again.

He moved within her and she wrapped her legs around him, seeking his rhythm, finding it, going with him. He tried to go slowly; she could feel him holding back, trying to make it last, to make it good for her sake.

She let him do that for a while, moving with measured care, not letting this heat between them get too out of hand. But she knew he couldn't last that way.

She didn't want him to. She wanted him wild and hungry and completely hers. She wanted him to give himself up to this wonder between them, as she had done, back there by the door.

She touched the side of his face. He braced up on his elbows again, his eyes burning into hers. "What?" The word was rough—still controlled, but barely.

She smiled at him. It was a brazen, knowing smile—and then she lifted her head and captured his mouth again, bucking against him at the same time.

That did it. With a guttural moan, he pushed into her hard. She took him, all of him, everything he could give.

After that, the world seemed to spin away into nothing but heat and wetness and mutual need. They rolled across the bed together, wild and so eager, holding on tight.

Finally he stiffened. She felt him pulsing into her. He threw back his head and pressed into her so deep. She held on tight, her own pleasure cresting, a thousand stars exploding behind her eyes.

For a time, they just lay there, still joined, arms and legs all tangled together, his breath warm and sweet across her cheek, the sweat of their lovemaking drying on their skin. It seemed she could feel his heart beating in time with hers, so fast at first and then gradually slowing.

He kissed her temple. "Cold?"

She smiled against his shoulder. "A little, I guess." Outside, the night was hot and close. But in the air-conditioned comfort of the Carsons' huge house, the temperature wasn't much over seventy.

"Come on. Let's get under the covers."

"Mmm." She rolled off the side of the bed and pulled back the coverlet. They both climbed in and he gathered her close again.

"Tired?"

She made a soft noise that meant yes and closed her eyes.

She came awake slowly. It probably wasn't that much later. The recessed overhead lights were still on, very low.

Flynt was touching her, stroking the side of her waist, cupping a breast, toying with it a little, then trailing that teasing hand downward, over her stomach—lower still.

She didn't even pretend to resist him. Why should she? She wanted him and he wanted her.

And more than that.

More than just wanting. More than just this physical hunger. More than desire.

She might as well say it, she realized. Might as well get it out there, tell him in words what she was pretty certain he already knew.

When he found the feminine heart of her, she moved against his hand, moaning his name on an exhalation of breath. "Flynt."

He made a low sound of masculine encouragement.

"Oh, Flynt."

He continued caressing her. She felt herself drifting off on a hot sea of pure sensation and she knew she must say the words, before words themselves were lost to her.

"Oh, Flynt, I love you. I love you so."

He lowered his mouth to hers, drank those words right off her lips. And down below, his fingers went on working their dangerous magic.

She would have told him again, cried she loved him out loud. But he had his mouth on hers and he was driving her crazy, driving her wild.

Just before she hit the peak, he reached for the box he'd set on the nightstand and he came into her, came with her, into that hot, spinning place where there was pure pleasure, an agony of glorious sensation. And then, at last, that final rising to the shattering wonder of shared fulfillment.

Flynt woke after sunrise. The heavy curtains were open. He hadn't thought to close them last night; now the room was bathed in morning light.

He didn't move. Not for a minute or two, anyway. Josie lay right there in the bed next to him, her velvety cheek cradled on his arm, her pale hair a sweet tangle against her white throat.

He thought of the night just past and his body hardened instantly. Ready for more.

She had said that she loved him.

He had liked hearing that. Liked it a lot. Liked it more, he supposed, than he had any right to like it.

More than he deserved. Yeah. That was Josie. A miracle in his life. And a hell of a lot more than he would ever deserve.

He glanced at the baby monitor. It sat on the nightstand next to the open box of condoms. There was a receiver in Josie's room, too—though this morning, there would be no one in her room to hear if Lena cried.

Flynt couldn't hold back a smile. Soon enough, Lena would cry. They'd have to get up and take care of her.

Carefully he slid his arm out from under Josie's

head. She let out a small sigh, turned her face the other way, but she didn't wake.

Good.

He took hold of the coverlet and slowly peeled it back.

Her body stole his breath. She was slim and her skin was smooth, her breasts as high and full as he remembered them. Her stomach was flat—concave, even, right now, as she lay on her back.

Not a stretch mark in sight that he could detect.

No difference, he thought, his mind spinning away from what that could mean. No difference at all....

Was that possible, after Lena? Could she have carried and delivered a baby and yet have her body show no signs that she had borne a child? It seemed damned unlikely.

Yet, who could say about something like that?

It could be. Certainly, it could be....

She woke right then, with no warning. She turned her head his way and those green eyes met his.

She knew instantly what he was up to. "Oh, Flynt." Her tone was chiding, her eyes sad.

He wanted to make demands. He wanted to force her, somehow, to tell him the truth.

But he had made a promise, and he would keep it. Lena's caseworker had said about two weeks. Twelve days had passed since he took the test. They'd have the undeniable truth very soon now.

She spoke again. "When will you believe me? Lena is not—"

He was not going to hear that. Tenderly he put his hand across her mouth, blocking her words. "No. Don't say it. Don't say it again."

He waited until she gave him a nod, then he let his hand slide away, down that silky white throat. "Kiss me," he commanded.

She lifted her mouth for him and he covered it with his own.

Thirteen

Lena woke about a half hour later. They went in together to feed and change her. Then Flynt called down to the kitchen to have breakfast sent up. They shared it at the table in the sitting room, with Lena rocking happily in her baby swing nearby.

When Lena went back to bed, so did they. For a couple of lovely, luxurious hours, they made love. It was slow and exciting, not quite so frantic as the night before.

In the afternoon, Josie showered and dressed to go check on her mother. Flynt tapped on her door just as she was putting on her lipstick. He'd showered and changed, too, into khakis and a polo shirt. He had Lena in his arms, all dressed in pink with a little pink bonnet on her head.

"We're coming with you," he announced.

"To my mother's?"

"That's right. Any objections?"

"Well, no. That would be fine." She felt a wide smile break over her face. "I'd love it."

So they all went to Alva's. Josie's mother seemed delighted to see them. She fed Lena her bottle, her eyes getting kind of misty. "Oh, it has been such a long, long time since I've held a sweet one like this in my arms."

If she had any questions about what, exactly, was going on between her daughter and Flynt Carson and the "mystery baby," she didn't ask them. She offered them sweet cold tea and some Toll House cookies she'd made the day before.

Flynt asked her how she was feeling.

"Much, much better. Good enough to bake cookies. That's something, don't you think?"

He agreed that it was—and he added that they were very good cookies. Just about the best he'd ever tasted, as a matter of fact.

Color came into Alva's too-pale cheeks. "I can see you are a charmer, Flynt Carson."

Flynt laughed at that. "'Charmer' is not the word most would use."

"Well, then, they probably don't know the real you."

They left Alva's around four. Josie lingered for a moment at the door, while Flynt, carrying Lena, went on ahead to his pickup, which was parked at the curb in front of the house.

"He's a keeper," her mother whispered. "Nothing like what everyone says."

Josie put on a disapproving expression. "Mama, have you been listening to gossip?"

"Well, now, honey, gossip is the thing we should

all be above—and also the thing that not many can resist.''

The two women fell silent. Flynt had reached the pickup. The afternoon sun brought out the streaks of gold in his hair. He opened the rear door and began hooking Lena into her seat.

Alva leaned close to Josie. ''Now that I've had a little time with him, I can see what you love in him. He's a good man.''

''Yes, he is.''

''You're gonna be happy.''

''I do hope so, Mama.'' She couldn't help remembering that morning, the way he had pulled the covers back as she slept and studied her body, looking for proof that she'd left her own baby on a golf course for him to find, that she'd lied to him and that she continued to lie.

No, things weren't settled yet. And there was no guarantee, when they were settled, that the outcome would be a happy one.

''I see those shadows in your eyes.'' Alva moved closer. Her lips brushed Josie's cheek. ''Remember. Follow your heart.''

''I'm trying, Mama. I truly am.''

They had their dinner in Lena's room. Then, as evening came on, they went outside and took a walk in the gardens at the back of the house, pushing Lena along the paths in a stroller.

Like the gardens at the club, the lush trees and flowers and the big expanses of lawn seemed almost too lovely to be real. South Texas, after all, was not naturally the greenest place on earth. Except near the rivers and along the coast, it was true brush country, the land as a rule rocky and dry, the vegetation heavy on cactus and bunch grass, good for raising cattle, and not much else.

It took a lot of water, doubtless out of nearby Lake Maria, to keep gardens like the ones around the Carson house green and beautiful. To Josie, it seemed just a tad wasteful. But it sure was a treat to stroll along in the inviting shade of the trees, enjoying the vivid beauty of a bougainvillea spilling down a trellis, admiring the roses that bloomed everywhere.

Beyond the gardens, she could see the roofs of all the buildings that made this a working ranch, barns and stables and housing for the hands. And beyond the outbuildings lay acres and acres of open country where the Carson cattle grazed.

Grace was waiting in Lena's room when they got back upstairs.

"The gardens are lovely," Flynt's mother said, the sweetest, warmest smile on her face. "I hope you've been enjoying them."

Both Josie and Flynt agreed that they had.

"Let me hold that little sweetheart." Grace scooped Lena into her arms. "I swear, if this is what it's like being a grandma, the job is for me. I want more grandchildren. And soon."

More, Grace had said. *I want* more *grandchildren.* Flynt's mother seemed so sure that Lena was his child.

Flynt didn't appear the least bothered by what his mother had just implied. He laughed. "You've got two daughters and two sons—and all of them are single as of today. It's not a promising start, Ma."

Grace said, "Well, we are working on the problem, now, aren't we?" She sounded very pleased.

And *that* did Josie's heart good. Cara really had gotten it right. She'd said Grace would come around.

"Now," Grace said, "I want you two to take the evening for yourselves. I'll watch Lena, practice my grandmothering skills." Josie and Flynt exchanged glances. Grace made a shooing motion with her hand. "Go on, now. I mean it. Have a lovely time."

"Well, Grace," Josie said, "if you're sure..."

"I'm positive."

Flynt took Josie's arm. "Let's get out of here before she has second thoughts."

"Good idea." They turned for the door.

Grace warned gently, "Don't stay out too late now."

Flynt promised, "We won't."

"And one more thing..."

They paused in the doorway. "Okay, Ma. What's the catch?"

Grace grinned. "Church. Tomorrow. Both of you. Be ready at ten. We'll all go together, as a family. I've already told your father and Cara. I'll make a point to speak with Matt and Fiona, as well."

"I'm on the golf course Sunday mornings. You know that."

"Not *this* Sunday, you're not."

"Where shall we go?" Flynt asked once they'd climbed into his fancy pickup and headed down the curving driveway that led to the road.

"How about the Saddlebag? I liked it there. It's cozy and quiet."

"Saddlebag it is."

They took the same table they'd had the night before and they held hands and leaned close and whispered to each other like the lovers they were.

"Your mother sure has changed her tune," Josie said.

"You noticed."

"I still can hardly believe that she wants me to go to church with you all. And I'll bet it's First Church, too, isn't it?"

"Right on both counts."

All the rich folks went to First Church. "Oh, I knew it. She's making a statement, isn't she? Letting the world know that she and your father have decided to accept me in your life."

"That's about the size of it. Does it bother you?"

"Aside from the jittery feeling in my stomach, I think it's just dandy. But it's too bad about your golf game."

"Yeah. That's a sacrifice, all right. But I suppose I'll bear up somehow."

"I'm so relieved to hear that."

"And as for your jittery stomach…"

"Yes?"

"Relax."

"That's real easy for you to say."

"I'm serious. Your biggest challenge will be staying awake during the sermon. Pastor Williams has one of those droning voices. Way too soothing. He needs a little more hellfire and brimstone in his delivery, to keep the sinners on their toes."

Josie couldn't hold back a giggle. "And you know we need it—with all the sinning we've been doing. And probably *will* be doing later tonight."

"No 'probably' about it."

Josie felt the blush creeping into her cheeks. "Your mother wouldn't approve."

"My mother will mind her own business now that she sees what direction we're headed in."

She wanted to ask him, "And what direction is that?" But she didn't quite dare. Not yet. In a way, everything seemed to hinge on those test results they were waiting for.

Once they came through and Flynt had accepted the truth, they could move on. They could talk about things like where they were going as a couple. They could make plans.

It was okay with Josie, really, that they weren't making plans right this minute. What they were doing was lovely, to be treasured for just what it was: two people holding hands across a table, talking and laughing and so glad to be together.

"Is that a slow song I hear?" He stood and pulled her up with him.

She went into his arms and they danced.

The hours went by so swiftly. It seemed as if hardly any time had passed, but according to the big heavily varnished wooden clock over the bar—the one carved in the shape of Texas—it was midnight. They agreed they should probably head back to the ranch to relieve Grace.

They found Flynt's mother in the same place as the night before—asleep in the rocker. They woke her gently. She said good-night.

Once she had left them, they went straight to Flynt's big bedroom and shut the door and did all the things that lovers do when they're finally alone together in the dark.

It was after three when they dropped off to sleep. Josie woke around seven, feeling marvelously well rested—and also as if she could eat a dozen eggs, a side of beef and maybe a loaf or two of Texas toast.

Flynt got a call on the house line from Matt about some ranch business that needed tending, so he left

her to take care of Lena and eat her big breakfast on
her own. He didn't return until nine-thirty. He jumped
in the shower to wash off the trail dust and was ready
just in time to head into town for the Carson family
visit to First Church.

They went in separate vehicles, Ford and Grace in
one of the Cadillacs, Josie, Lena and Flynt in his big
pickup, Matt in his pickup and Fiona and Cara each
in cars of their own.

"No such thing as carpooling in the Carson family," Josie teased as they drove into town.

Flynt grunted. "No way. We all need to know
we've got a means of escape, if it comes to that."

Josie made a scoffing sound. "Oh, come on. Going
to church together can't be that bad."

"You're right. It's not. Truth is, we Carsons are all
independent types. We like to get places on our own
steam."

She sent him a musing look.

He glanced over and frowned. "What?"

"Well, and yet you all still live out at the ranch."

He shrugged. "Yeah, but on our own terms. Matt
has his house. So does Cara. My wing is pretty much
the same as having my own place. Fiona's the only
one who lives in my parents' part of the house. But
her rooms are *her* rooms and both our parents respect
that—for the most part, anyway."

Josie picked up on the operative phrase. "For the
most part?"

"Yeah. When it comes to Fiona, my father's on the verge of— How should I put it? Interfering in her life, I guess you could say."

"Because?"

"She's so damned wild. He thinks she'll never settle down. Both he and Ma worry she'll get herself into some scrape she can't get out of. In case you didn't notice, she is spoiled. Running around from one guy to the next. And it's kind of terrifying, the way she can spend money. My dad's been making noises lately that he's going to have to do something to rein her in."

"Flynt, come on. Fiona can wrap your father around her little finger."

"Right. But that doesn't mean he's not worried for her, that he isn't thinking she needs to change her ways—and that if she won't change on her own, he'll just have to help her along."

"How would he do that?"

"Hell if I know. I don't think *he* knows, yet."

At the church, they took Lena to the nursery and then joined the rest of the family for the service. Cara, as always, was warm and friendly. Ford, in his gruff way, made sure Josie knew he welcomed her presence. Grace was a sweetheart.

Matt was quiet and kind of brooding, as if he had something weighing on his mind. Josie had a pretty good idea of what. She couldn't help hurting for him and for Rose.

Fiona batted her eyelashes and patted the space next to her in the family pew. "Sit right here, Josie Lavender, and tell me all about how you've been. I swear, you just vanished last year, now didn't you? Pouf. You were gone, gone, gone."

Grace said, "Now, Fiona..."

But Josie only grinned. "Great to see you, too, Fiona. I've been doin' fine, really. Living up near Dallas. But my mama's not well so I had to come home."

"I'll tell you this much." Fiona cast a meaningful glance in Flynt's direction. "Some people sure seem pleased to have you around again."

Flynt was sitting on Josie's other side. She felt his hand brushing hers, then clasping it. She gave his fingers a squeeze and told Fiona softly, "Well, it is good to be home."

After the service Fiona and Matt made excuses and took off, as Flynt had predicted a few of the Carsons might. The rest of them hung around to shake hands with Pastor Williams out on the wide church steps beneath the already punishing late-morning sun.

Grace introduced Josie. "Pastor Williams, this is Josie Lavender. She is a...very close friend of Flynt's."

"Delighted to meet you, my dear," said the pastor. Josie shook his hand, which was long and thin and dotted with age spots.

"We'll go on out to the club now," Grace announced after Josie and Flynt had collected the baby. "For brunch in the Empire Room."

Cara spoke up. "You four go on. I'll get Flynt to put the baby seat in my car and take Lena home with me."

"Oh, honey, are you sure?" Grace asked the question, but clearly only for the sake of form.

"Absolutely."

Grace turned to Flynt and Josie. "Well, now. What do you two say to that?"

Flynt leaned close to Josie. "Do you get the feeling we couldn't get out of brunch if we tried?"

Josie elbowed him in the ribs and told his mother, "Brunch in the Empire Room sounds just great."

At Harvey Small's recommendation, they all had eggs Benedict. That time he didn't steer them wrong. The sauce was smooth and tasty, the eggs poached to perfection. They had fresh-squeezed orange juice, too, and the coffee was excellent. Josie couldn't quite finish hers, after the huge breakfast she'd eaten earlier, but she gave it her best effort, because it all tasted so good.

Josie spotted Rose at a table halfway across the room, with a woman Josie thought she recognized as Kate Wainwright, Rose's mother. Kate and Archy Wainwright, Rose's father, didn't enjoy the kind of marital contentment that Grace and Ford shared. They had divorced years ago.

Rose caught Josie's eye when no one was looking. The two women shared a quick nod of mutual acknowledgment. After that, Josie took care not to look Rose's way again, lest she somehow betray the secret she had sworn to keep.

As on Friday night, people kept dropping by the table. Either Grace or Ford would always make a point of introducing Josie. Josie would smile and say hello. There would be a moment or two more of casual chatting, and whoever it was would move on.

Judge Bridges, the tall, white-haired fellow who had represented Flynt and his buddies when Haley Mercado drowned, came over, too. As soon as Grace determined that he was alone, she insisted he join them. The judge didn't have to be asked twice. A waiter brought him a chair and a place setting and he said he would try the eggs Benedict, too.

"And how is the 'mystery baby' doing?" he asked as he smoothed the snowy-white monogrammed napkin across his lap.

That set Grace off on what a darling Lena was. Such a sweet baby, a happy baby. A good eater, too. "I swear, she's grown an inch since she's been with us. Oh, and when that little beauty smiles, the world is a brighter place and that is no lie...."

Judge Bridges turned his white head Josie's way. "I think I heard that you're the one taking care of her?"

Josie nodded. "Grace is right. She's a darling."

Grace gushed some more. "It's just like a gift, really, to have her with us. You know how I am. I've been longing for grandchildren. It's so wonderful to think I'm a grandma at last."

The judge blinked. "Ah. Is that right? It's official, then?"

Grace frowned. "Official?"

"Ahem. Well. I understood there were some…test results pending."

"That's right," Flynt said in a patient tone.

"And?"

"No, Carl. The results haven't come through yet."

"Ah."

Grace waved a plump hand. "Oh, that. I'd forgotten all about that. We expect them any time now, don't we, Flynt?"

"Yeah, Ma. We do."

"And what's next?" the judge asked. "When you finally know for certain, either way?"

Josie felt Flynt's eyes on her. She turned to him, met his gaze head-on and gave him a steady smile. He said, quietly, "We'll have to get back to you on that, Carl."

"Long as I'm the first to know."

Monday morning, Flynt woke before Josie.

He indulged himself for a minute or two, just lying there next to her, thinking that damned if this wasn't just how life should be. A man should fall asleep at night exhausted from good loving with the right woman. When he woke in the morning, that woman should be there, beside him, her silvery hair all tangled on the pillow, a tiny, contented smile on her soft mouth. His sheets should smell of her, of soap and flowers and that indefinable sweetness that only her skin gave off.

He wanted to wake her with kisses and slow caresses, but he'd been loafing too much the past couple of days. He had a pile of things to do in his study and he had to get over to the club for lunch with a couple of cattlemen from Laredo.

Besides, for once, the monitor on the nightstand was silent. Might as well let the woman sleep until Lena woke and started making her demands.

Carefully he pushed the covers aside and slid from the bed. He tiptoed to his walk-in closet, got what he needed and headed for his bathroom.

Twenty minutes later he emerged, showered, shaved and fully dressed. In the bed, Josie slept on. He resisted the urge to bend down, brush a kiss on her cheek and another against her smooth throat.

He went to his study and had his breakfast brought up to him there. He worked until noon and stopped by Lena's room on his way out to meet with the men from Laredo.

He held the baby. He kissed his woman. And then he headed for the club.

He returned to the ranch at a little after four and

found Cara with the baby—which he'd more or less expected. At that time of day, Josie was usually gone for her visit with her mother.

He paused in the doorway just long enough to let Cara know he'd returned. "I'll be in my study. Tell Josie I'm there when she gets back in?"

"I'll let her know you're waiting for her."

"Yeah," he said, and knew he had the grin of a ridiculously happy man on his face. "Do that."

In his study, he found a pile of mail to get through. Anita had left it where she always did, on the ebony tray table just inside the door. He grabbed up the stack of envelopes and circulars and carried it all to his desk to deal with in a while. The cattlemen from Laredo had given him a few ideas for improvement in the Carson breeding program. He had some figures he wanted to check right away, while it was all still fresh in his mind.

He'd brought up the spreadsheet program on his laptop and was just settling in for some serious number crunching when the phone rang—the outside line.

He picked it up. "Flynt Carson."

"Hello, Mr. Carson. It's Eliza Guzman."

Lena's caseworker. Flynt snapped to attention in his chair. "Yeah. Hi. How are you?"

"I'm doing well, thanks. I received the results of your test today. You should have them, too, I'd imagine. We need to discuss what we want to do next."

"Next?" he echoed. What did that mean?

"Yes. Where do we go from here? That's the question, and we need to come up with some answers."

"Oh. Right." He grabbed the pile of envelopes off his desk and started going through them. "I don't…just a minute…"

"Sure." The social worker waited.

He found the envelope—a full-size FedEx letter mailer. Which shouldn't have surprised him, as he'd arranged to have the test results sent to him that way. He had a lot of stuff sent via courier, though, so the damn thing hadn't stood out in the pile.

All at once, his mouth had a dry, coppery taste. He wanted a drink—more than *wanted*. In fact, the need was so intense at that moment, it almost doubled him over.

He tore off the strip that sealed the mailer shut, reached in and took out the smaller envelope inside. It, too, was sealed shut. He slid back his chair, yanked open the pencil drawer, got out a letter opener and sliced the envelope along the top fold.

He ripped out the single sheet of paper inside, read it over quickly, then read it again. And again.

After three times through, he began to accept what it said—that there was no possibility Lena could be his child.

Fourteen

Not his.

Lena was not his.

"Mr. Carson?"

"Uh, yeah. Right here."

"You did receive the letter from the lab, then?"

"Yeah. Got it."

"You understand what it—"

"Yeah. I've read it."

"Well," said the social worker. "Then you can see why I've called. Most likely, at this point, you'll want me to come and pick up the child. We have several options for her care and—"

"What options?" he growled into the phone.

"Well, foster care, actually. We have a sort of halfway house she can go to right away and—"

"A halfway house."

"Yes."

"You're saying there's no one, really, to take her."

"Well, until we can discover who the real parents are, we'll just have to—"

"She stays here."

There was dead silence from the other end of the line.

Flynt realized that, perhaps, barking orders was not the best way to handle this. He gentled his tone. "I mean, if we can work it out, I think it would be best for Lena to remain here. Until we can...find out more, find out who she belongs to." He thought of Tyler. Of Spence. And Michael.

And Luke, damn it. Still off somewhere. As far as Flynt knew, no one had seen Luke Callaghan in several weeks now.

Flynt went on, polite but insistent, "It makes the most sense, don't you think? You've already approved things here at the ranch, and Lena seems happy here."

There was another silence. Then the social worker said, "Well, that really might be best. If you're sure that would work for you...."

He saw Lena's sweet, round face in his mind, those blue eyes he'd been telling himself she got from him. "I'm sure."

"I'll need to schedule a home visit right away, so I can note that the child is being well cared for. A matter of form, that's all. But necessary."

"No problem."

"Tomorrow, then? Say, around nine in the morning? Will that do?"

"Yes. Nine is good."

The social worker said goodbye. He set the phone down.

He tried to go back to the spreadsheet, but it was no good. None of those columns of figures meant a damn thing to him right then. He shut it down.

After that, he just sat there, wanting a drink. And waiting for Josie to knock on the door.

Holding a finger to her lips, Cara rose from the rocker. She tiptoed from the baby's room and joined Josie in the hallway, pulling the door silently shut behind her.

Josie spoke softly. "How long has she been down?"

"Maybe half an hour." Cara grinned. "I'd say you've got a little time to yourself."

"Wonderful. Where's Flynt?" Just saying his name caused something hot and sweet to flare inside her.

"In his study."

"He's probably working and doesn't want to be interrupted."

Cara was giving her that teasing grin. "That would depend on who interrupted him."

"Well," Josie said, grinning right back, "you think he'll be glad to see me?"

"I know he will."

Josie stopped in her own room for a minute, to put her purse away and grab the receiver for the baby monitor. Then she went on down the hall to the room at the end, right across from his bedroom. She tapped twice on the door.

From the other side, she heard his voice. "It's open."

His desk faced the door. He was sitting behind it, a pile of unopened mail and his shut laptop in front of him. He appeared to be doing nothing.

"Flynt?" Something was wrong. He sat too still. And the way he stared at her...

The warmth inside faded, to be replaced by a chill that slithered along beneath the surface of her skin. Prickly and frightening.

"Flynt?"

"Come in. Shut the door."

She did as he instructed, then found herself hovering there, her back against the door, her stomach in a hard, cold knot. "What has happened?"

"Come here."

Suddenly she was thinking of that night last summer. That night she brought him his dinner—into this very room—and he grabbed her hand, almost grinding the bones. And he pulled her close and kissed her.

And then carried her to his bed.

But no. There might be a similar intensity radiating from him as on that night, but it wasn't the same. That wasn't unsatisfied desire she saw in his eyes. It was something much darker and much more complex.

He picked up a white sheet of paper from the desk. "Here. Look."

She knew then. Even before she made herself go to him and take the paper from his hand, even before she read over the proof of what she'd been trying to get him to see for two weeks now.

She set the letter on the desk, put the baby monitor on top of it and made herself meet his eyes.

He said, "So. You weren't lying." It sounded like an accusation.

What had she expected? She had known all along that when he finally had to face the truth about this, it would be very tough.

She restated the facts, keeping her voice calm and low. "I told you I wasn't lying. I told you over and over. You wouldn't believe me. Even though I think you know I am no liar."

He looked at her for a long bleak moment. Then he muttered, "Yeah. I know." He shoved his chair back.

She flinched at the sudden, violent movement. She was, after all, Rutger Lavender's daughter. Where she came from, when a man made a fast, angry move, it was usually a good idea to get out of his way.

She flinched—but she held her ground. Flynt was not her daddy, thank God. Flynt would never raise his hand to a woman.

He didn't come toward her. He paced around the

other side of the big desk and then stopped with his back to her.

She waited. She didn't have anything that terrific to say right then, anyway.

Finally he turned her way again. "I wanted to think that Lena was your one lie. Your only lie. A lie I could forgive you, given the circumstances."

"I know that," she said softly.

"Then why, knowing that the truth would come out soon enough, did you come back here? Why the hell didn't you just stay away? Why did you have to start in with me all over again, put us through this all over again?"

"Flynt. I told you why. I told you from the first. Because I wanted another chance with you. Because I'm good with children, and that baby in the other room needed someone like me. Because I saw the look in your eyes that night when you came knocking on my bedroom window at my mama's house. You *wanted* Lena to be ours, wanted it so much that it gave me hope, gave me the will to fight for your heart."

He was shaking his head. "I told you, Josie. Loud and clear. There is no chance with me. There never was a chance with me."

She couldn't let him get away with that one. "Oh, yes, there was. If that letter had said Lena was ours, you'd be asking me to marry you right now, and we both know it."

He was silent—for a few weighted seconds, anyway, in deference to the truth in her words. But then he said, "Lena is not ours."

"That's right." Josie stood tall, kept her head high. "So take a big risk. Ask me to marry you, anyway."

He only looked at her, his face carefully composed and his eyes somewhere else, somewhere far away in a place she could never go.

She forged on. "All right. Don't ask me. I'll ask you." She came around the end of the desk and started toward him.

"Josie, stop."

But she didn't stop. She marched right up to him and she dropped on one knee, snaring his hand. "Flynt Carson, I love you. I want to spend my life with you. I want to have your babies and raise those babies, watch them grow strong and tall. I want…the two of us. I want what we are and what we can be. What we can build together if we stand side by side. I want my hope fulfilled and my dreams to come true. If you say yes, it will be a big step in that direction. So, will you please marry me?"

He was looking down at her. But he wasn't saying yes. Nothing about him said yes. He tugged on the hand she held. "Get up, Josie. Please."

Something happened in her heart then—a sort of shrinking feeling. She was getting nowhere. She was down on her knees and his answer was still no.

His answer was and always would be no.

So who was the fool here? Who was the pitiful, deluded fool?

She let go of his hand and stood. "It was a big step for you, to give up drinking," she said quietly. "To live your life straight. But you're still not really living, Flynt Carson. Not until you give up that guilt you carry around with you like it was something so precious, so sacred, so special."

He didn't say anything. He wore a tired, patient expression, as if he was only waiting for her to run out of words.

She hadn't. Not yet. "You wear your guilt like a medal, Flynt. It means more to you than that Silver Star you won in the war. It means more to you than I do. A whole lot more. More to you than—"

"Stop." His voice was ice-cold. "Just stop. Let it go, Josie."

"No, I won't. I will have my say, even though I can see in your eyes that I've lost this fight. That I never had a chance—not unless I'd had your baby, not unless you could believe you had a duty to marry me. Oh, now, you think about that. Now that is just plain crazy, if you ask me. You would marry me for duty's sake but not because you love me. Not because you know that together we could be something really good—and you do know that, don't you?"

"Josie—"

"Just say it. Just admit it. We could be the kind of partners married people ought to be. We could build us a fine life, a life with room for lots of children, children who could grow up and give back to this world.''

He uttered her name again, his voice low and ragged.

"Say it, Flynt. Say that you know it.''

He tried to turn from her.

She didn't let him. She grabbed his arm, pulled him back around. "Say it.''

"All right, damn you.'' He shook off her hand and then confessed roughly, "I know it. Now, are you satisfied?''

"No. No, I am not satisfied. How could I be? To give yourself permission to love me only for duty's sake, that is so...sad and crazy. That is plain wrong. That is right next-door to evil, Flynt Carson. You have to see that.''

He opened his mouth to say something, then shut it and looked away. "You don't understand.''

"Well, fine. If I don't, then you explain it to me. You make me understand.''

"Monica *knew,* damn it.'' The words seemed to come from him of their own accord.

"What?''

He said it again, flatly this time. "Monica knew.''

"What? She knew what?''

"That I...that I had...noticed you. That you were there, in the back of my mind. She knew it before I knew it. She knew it that night. The night that she died. That's what she was mad about, what we fought about in the car. She said she didn't like the way I looked at you. She said there she was, fat and ugly, giving me the baby I wanted so much, and I was looking at the housekeeper.''

"But that's not true, Flynt. You know it's not. I was the housekeeper and that's all I ever was to you until a long time after Monica was gone.''

He waved a hand. "I told her she was nuts. And you're right, at the time I believed it myself, believed I hadn't so much as looked in your direction. I remember how I felt. Self-righteous and furious that she would dare to accuse me of putting moves on the household help.''

"So you did tell her, right? You told her she had it wrong?''

His mouth twisted bleakly. "That's what I should have said. Gently, reasonably. Or I should have said nothing, till later. I should have kept silent while I was driving that car on that cold winter's night on that very icy road. But I didn't. I said, 'Damn it, Monica. You are off your rocker. You are certifiably nuts.'''

Josie shook her head.

Flynt shrugged. "I know. Seriously bad move. It just made her madder. She called me a bastard and grabbed the steering wheel.''

"Oh, God,'' Josie whispered.

"You know the rest. And you know how it turned out. That I wanted you, after all. That she was right."

"Flynt, it's what you *did* that matters. And you did nothing. Nothing. You never so much as looked at me. You didn't. Not till long after Monica was dead."

"I just can't…it stays with me. That she wouldn't have died if I hadn't been so damn self-righteous about the whole thing. She'd be alive and so would the baby."

"Would she?"

He gave her a dark look. "What is that supposed to mean?"

"Just that you can't know what would have happened if you could go back. You can't go back. You can only live now. And if you don't live now, you might as well be in the grave with your dead wife and that poor little baby that never even got to be born."

He turned away again.

She thought she had already accepted the fact that she'd lost him. Still, it was like a knife turning inside her when he said, "I'm sorry, Josie. Whatever excuses you try to make for me, I can't accept them. It's not going to work. I want you to go." He turned on his heel and went back to the desk, where he pulled one of those big professional-size checkbooks out of a drawer, grabbed a pen and filled out a check. He tore the thing off and held it out. "Here's what I owe you. Go home to your mama. Make yourself a decent life. Find a decent guy.''

Josie stared at that check, knowing she should have at least been a little bit prepared for what was happening. But somehow, she hadn't. She'd imagined that it would be rough, yes. But in her heart she'd been certain love would win in the end. That it would all work out to a sweet happily-ever-after for the two of them.

Naive, that was what both Flynt and Rose Wainwright had called her. She guessed they were right.

An awful wave of pure hopelessness washed over her.

But then he waved the check at her. ''Here. Take it.''

And despair became something that felt a lot like anger. ''Just like that, huh?''

''Josie—''

''Just take that check, walk out of this room, get my things and go?''

''Look, you know it's the best way.''

Well, and here we are all over again, she thought. Just like before. Guilt is the winner. He hands me a check and I get the heck out.

Forget that.

Maybe he refused to get past the tragedy of losing a wife and child. But *she* had learned a thing or two since the last time he sent her away. Darned if she'd go slinking off like some kind of criminal, like she had to feel as guilty as he did. She had nothing to feel guilty about, except for the "crime" of loving Flynt Carson.

He was looking pained. And he'd been holding out the check for long enough that it was getting pretty awkward. He set it on the edge of the desk.

"Josie, take the damn check. This is money you earned, money I owe you. I'm just settling up, giving you what is yours."

"No." She said it loud and she said it clear.

He glowered. "There's no point in stringing this out. I've said it can't work between us, that I want you to—"

"And I said no. Not right yet. There's more than just the two of us to think about this time. Maybe you've forgotten. There's also Lena."

"Lena," he repeated, as if he didn't know what she was getting at.

So she told him. "Even if Lena isn't our baby girl, she is still going to need someone to look after her until her real mama can be found."

"I'm aware of that, damn it."

"Oh, well, that's nice. You mean you're not just going to put her back in her car seat and leave her on the golf course for someone else to find?"

"Of course not. I've already talked to her case-worker. Lena will stay right here until we can figure out who her parents are."

"Fine. Then you'll need to hire a new nanny."

He looked at her sideways. "Okay. So?"

"So I'll stay until you do—and don't you even give me that look, Flynt Carson. This is no last-ditch effort to get you to see what we could have together. I am done, get it? I got your message loud and clear this time. I won't be chasing after you ever again. But I won't be run off like some thief in the night, either. I'll stay—for Lena's sake—until you can find another nanny. And you, I'll ignore. All I ask is that you do the same for me."

Fifteen

"So what now?" asked Tyler. He tightened the towel around his waist and let his head drop back against the cobalt-blue wall tiles of the men's steam room.

Flynt blotted moisture from his face. He'd decided it was time for a meeting and he'd called them all together—well, Tyler, Spence and Michael, anyway. Luke was still gone who the hell knew where.

Flynt said, "First off, I'd suggest you three set up paternity tests." He squinted through the clouds of steam. "Contact Eliza Guzman at Child Protective Services. She's Lena's caseworker. She can probably set up the tests."

Spence nodded. "Eliza Guzman. Got it." Tyler and Michael made noises of agreement.

"Anyone seen Luke lately?"

The men looked at each other and shook their heads. Tyler said, "Sunday, it was me and Spence. Luke was a no-show again." He gave Flynt a mock-scowl. "And no thanks to you, we had to wait around the clubhouse for an extra half hour to pick up two more players."

"Sorry." Flynt looked away. He didn't want to think about last Sunday. Last Sunday he'd gone to church with Josie and Lena. Last Sunday he'd been a happy man.

Spence asked, "What about the baby?"

"She's still at the ranch." Flynt spiked his fingers back through his wet hair. "It seemed like the best way to go for now—give her some consistency, some margin of stability until we can track down her parents."

Josie was still at the ranch, too, looking after Lena as she'd insisted on doing, until they could find someone suitable to take over for her. She was also keeping her word and keeping clear of him. When he came in the baby's room, she would leave. She only spoke to him when she absolutely had to, to say things like, "Here's the bottle" or "Buzz me when you're ready to go and I'll take over."

It was driving him just a little bit insane, having her right there, so close—and yet completely out of his reach. He couldn't touch. They hardly spoke.

But he was getting through it. He was managing. It hadn't been all that long, really, just three days since their confrontation in his study—three days.

It only seemed like forever.

Grace was supposed to be finding Josie's replacement. However, a good nanny, evidently, wasn't all that easy to find.

Or so Grace kept telling him.

But he felt certain it wouldn't be long now. She would find someone soon. Josie would be gone and he would be—well, not free of her, exactly. That wouldn't happen for a long time to come. Hell, if he wanted to be brutally honest, he might as well admit that it might never happen. But at least he wouldn't have to see her every day, to have her look right through him, to long to reach out and know he couldn't. To face the fact, day by day, hour by hour, that even if his control broke again, hers wouldn't.

She was firm against him now. He could see it in the determined set of her shoulders, in the tone of her voice, so disconnected and cool, whenever she had no choice but to speak to him. She was cut off from him, closed to him in some elemental and permanent way.

The loss was like a big, ugly hole in the center of himself.

Michael said, "Nobody's coming forward on this, damn it. If we don't take some action, that little girl will be walking and talking before anyone finds out who she belongs to."

"I talked to Hart O'Brien at MCPD day before yesterday," Flynt told them. His conversation with the detective had been brief and to the point. "He said he was backing out of it, that the sheriff's office was taking full jurisdiction over the investigation. He also said that since I've been eliminated as the father, you guys can expect to be hearing from the sheriff some time soon."

"Great," said Michael. "And what does that mean?"

Spence chuckled. "It means the case is still open and they'll call us when they want to talk to us."

Michael toweled sweat from his brow. "Maybe we need to step up to the plate here, help things along a little."

Spence was nodding. "You're right. We need to get somebody on this ourselves."

"Maybe Ben Ashton?" Tyler suggested.

Flynt recognized the name. Ashton was a private investigator with his own small agency over in Corpus.

"He's good," said Spence. "Want me to give him a call? We could put him on the paternity tests, instead of having the caseworker handle it."

The others exchanged glances. Then Flynt nodded. "Go for it."

"I could use a drink," Tyler said after they'd all showered and dressed. "How about it?"

Flynt probably should have begged off. But then what? It was five-thirty on Thursday night. He had no dinner plans, nothing to do but go home.

Where Josie was.

He went with the others into the temporary Men's Grill and ordered his usual, though he was seriously tempted to do otherwise.

Not that being tempted was anything new.

It was only that lately, the past few days, the yearning for a good, stiff drink had gotten so much stronger—and more frequent. Lately he thought about Josie all the time and that hurt. And when he hurt, he wanted something to kill the pain.

He knew just what would do it. It came in liquid form.

So far he was holding on to sobriety. But every day he had to be around Josie and not touch her or even really talk to her, he found himself wondering—more often and more strongly—what the hell difference it made if he stayed sober or not.

Harvey appeared at the table and fawned over them for a minute or two. Then something happened over by the waitress station. The little redhead, Erica, got into it with Daisy Parker—the new one, that dark-eyed blonde. A couple of drinks went flying from a tray, glass shattering and booze soaking the carpet. Erica looked as if she might claw the blonde's eyes out. The blonde, though, stood right up to her. Clearly Daisy Parker was a woman who knew how to hold her own.

Before much more could happen, Harvey got on the case. He headed right over there and led the two women off—presumably for a lecture in his office. About twenty minutes later, they all reappeared. The waitresses went back to work, and Harvey hustled off to greet another group of men who'd just arrived in the Grill.

Flynt thought about calling Harvey over and telling him what Josie had witnessed Friday concerning the redhead and Frank Del Brio. But then what? After the scene with Daisy Parker, Erica wouldn't be in Harvey's good graces. If he said something negative about her right now, she'd no doubt be looking for work.

And what was it Josie had said?

Even a mean girl's gotta eat...

He felt a smile pull at the corner of his mouth as he remembered. They'd been at the Saddlebag, Friday night, holding hands across the cocktail table. She'd leaned close and insisted that she didn't want Erica Clawson fired.

And then a slow song had come on the jukebox and he'd taken her into his arms....

Spence elbowed him lightly in the ribs.

Flynt shook himself. "Yeah?"

Spence leaned close and tipped his head in Daisy Parker's direction. "Something familiar about that blonde, don't you think?"

Before Flynt could answer, one of the other waitresses came by and asked them if they were ready for another round.

When the waitress left the table, James Campbell, a local attorney, came by. Campbell was getting married in a couple of weeks.

"Congratulations, man," said Tyler.

"Have a seat," Spence offered.

"Why not? I've got time for a drink."

Campbell took a chair across the table. The waitress returned. Flynt sipped his club soda and answered when spoken to and tried not to see Josie's face in his mind, not to hear her voice in his head....

It was a little after five when Josie came in from her daily visit to her mama's house. She found Grace in the rocker feeding Lena her bottle.

Flynt's mother looked up. "Ah. There you are." She smiled the sweetest, warmest of smiles. "Now, doesn't this girl have a big appetite?"

"Yes, she does. How did the interviews go today?"

"Well, now, Josie, there were no real prospects today. The two that agency sent over, well, one seemed downright sulky. And the other was a stiff one, you know? Can't have someone stuffy and mean looking after our Lena, now can we?"

Josie knew a runaround when she heard one. "Grace, we're going to have to talk."

"Yes, dear?"

"You know, don't you, that Flynt wants me out of here?"

Grace frowned. "Now, we both know that's not true. My son—"

"Grace." Josie crossed the room and knelt before Grace and the baby. "Listen."

Grace arranged her face into serious lines. "Of course."

"I am so sorry about all this, I truly am."

Another frown creased Grace's brow. "Oh, now, don't. You've nothing to feel sorry for. If anyone should apologize, I imagine I should. I was hasty in my judgment at first. And, well, I suppose I have to admit, I behaved like something of a snob."

Josie felt more than a little bit teary-eyed. She put her hand over Grace's. "We worked through it."

"Yes, we did."

"And then, no sooner did you get used to the idea of Flynt and me together than it was over."

"Well, now, maybe it's *not* over."

"Grace, it's over. I promise you. You know he thought that Lena was mine? And his?"

A faint blush tinged Grace's soft cheek. She looked down at the baby she held in her arms. "Ford and I, we did put two and two together. We thought that you must have left last year because something had happened between you and Flynt."

"You're right. Something did happen."

Grace looked up then. "I thought so."

"But I didn't have Lena. Lena is not mine. And she's not Flynt's."

Grace sighed. "Yes, I know. Flynt explained all about that test he took and what it proved. I must admit, I'm very disappointed." She looked at Lena again, her eyes soft with affection. "There's nothing

I'd love more than to have this little one call me Grandma.''

''I know. But she's not your grandbaby and she's not Flynt's daughter. And the truth is, he only planned to marry me because he thought she was.''

Grace made a sound of pure outrage. ''That is ridiculous.'' She spoke so strongly, it surprised the baby. Lena popped off the bottle, blue eyes wide. ''Oh,'' said Grace. ''Oh, now. It's okay.'' She guided the bottle back into the tiny mouth and Lena started sucking away. Then Grace spoke more quietly—but still with some heat. ''That is pure idiocy. I may get things wrong now and then, but basically I know my own son. Flynt has come to love you. And I have seen you together. I know you love him, too.''

''Love isn't the problem.''

''Then it will work out. You'll see. In the end the two of you will—''

''No, Grace. We won't.''

''But—''

''Please. It really isn't right for me to say any more. Except to tell you that Flynt and I truly are through.'' Josie put a light hand on Lena's warm brow, brushed at the feathery wisps of dark hair. ''I have only stayed on here because I feel a responsibility to this baby, because I didn't want to do what I did last year—just vanish and leave you scrambling to find someone to fill my job. I wanted to give you a few days to replace me. But now I see you're really not looking, are you, Grace?''

Grace's gaze slid away.

Josie prompted gently. ''Are you?''

Grace looked at her full on. ''All right. No, I haven't been. I've been…hoping. I've been thinking that if you two only had a little time…''

''Sorry. But time won't do it. It's over, Grace. It's done. I want to go home. And Flynt needs for me to go home. I will miss you all a lot, but that's the way it has to be.''

Grace looked at her for a long time, her blue eyes shining with not-quite-shed tears. ''You would have made a fine wife for him. For a few days there, I was so happy, Josie, to think that it had happened at last. Love for Flynt. He hasn't had an easy life, you know. Not really. You should have known him as a child. He was a charmer, so sweet and so carefree. But then so much went wrong for him.''

''I know. And I'm sorry.''

''You are the wife he needs, the woman he should have married in the first place.''

Josie found she was smiling. ''Well, considering I was only about fifteen when he met Monica, and that the Carsons and the Lavenders don't hang out with the same crowd, that just didn't happen.''

''It should have—and don't you do it, Josie Lavender.''

''Do what?''

"Give me another of your little lectures concerning the word 'should.' I don't need to hear it. Much as it pains me, I know that you're right. If you must go, then I'm not the one to stop you."

"So, you'll find someone, soon?"

Grace balanced the bottle against her generous bosom and quickly swiped the tears away. "You might have noticed that I did conduct a few interviews, just to keep up appearances."

"Yes, I did notice."

Grace sniffed. "And one of the women I talked to, I believe will work out fine. I'll go call her now, ask her if she can start tomorrow."

"Oh, Grace. I will miss you." Josie got to her feet.

Careful of her fragile burden, Grace rose from the rocker. "No one says you have to be a stranger."

It was a lovely thing to say. But a continued friendship with Grace wasn't to be, and Josie knew it. Flynt wanted her out of his life. He didn't want to have to see her. She understood, really, because she felt the same. It just plain hurt too much to be near him.

Grace said, "Here. Take this angel, will you? I'll make that call."

Sixteen

Josie left Carson Ranch the next day.

She worked until two, showing the new nanny what she needed to know, and then she went home to the little yellow house where her mother lived. She put her clothes away in her old chest of drawers and she hooked up her computer. Then she went over to the Mission Creek Café and asked for her old job back.

Gus Andros hired her on the spot. "You start tomorrow, seven to three."

"I'll be here."

She bought a pizza on the way home and she and her mama ate it in the living room while they watched her mama's favorite, *Law and Order*.

"You gonna be okay, honey?" Alva asked softly after her program was over.

"It hurts, Mama. It hurts a lot. But I am gonna be fine."

Friday night when Flynt went to check on Lena, the new nanny was there. He had known she would be.

Grace had told him she'd found someone. "She's

caring and bright, and she comes with fine references. She's not Josie, but then, nobody is.''

"Great, Ma. Thanks.''

Grace was not pleased with him and she couldn't resist telling him so. "That's all you've got to say? You've gone and thrown away the best thing that ever—"

"Ma, don't start on me.''

She'd pursed up her mouth and glared at him, but at least she shut up.

When he came in Friday night, he and the new nanny exchanged pleasantries. Then he told her to take a break. He'd look after Lena for an hour or two.

He fed Lena and diapered her and told her a silly story. Not that she understood it. But it cheered him a little, to watch her laugh and wave her arms around. He couldn't get enough of that smile of hers. And when he held her, for a moment or two he almost succeeded in forgetting that Josie was gone and she wasn't coming back.

At seven, he gave Lena to the nanny and he went downstairs to the main wing and joined his mother, his father, Cara and Matt for dinner. Fiona was off somewhere—getting herself in trouble, probably.

It was not a pleasant meal. His parents and Cara were all good and mad at him. Josie had worked her special magic on them and they had accepted her, were beginning to think of her as part of the family. Now they'd lost her—again. Even if they didn't have all the details, they knew that he was the reason she was gone.

Matt was even worse than the others. Something was eating him, had been for a while now. He was surly in general lately. But with Flynt that evening he crossed the line into outright belligerence.

Right after they all sat down, he said, "I hear Josie's gone." He glared right at Flynt.

Flynt nodded and kept his face a blank. "That's right."

"I thought you had something good going with her."

No way Flynt was getting into that. "She's gone. That's all you need to know. Would you mind passing the salt?"

Matt muttered something so low Flynt couldn't quite make it out, picked up the saltshaker and shoved it Flynt's way.

Flynt just didn't get it. Matt hardly knew Josie, really. Why the hell should he get all worked up because it hadn't worked out between her and his brother?

But Matt was worked up.

And whatever was eating him, he'd decided to exercise his frustrations on Flynt.

He started in with complaints—about a certain land deal Flynt had gotten them into that hadn't quite worked out the way they'd all hoped it might. About some damn special feed orders. Matt said they'd been shorted and someone had to look into it.

Flynt tried to keep his cool, but he wasn't feeling any too even-tempered himself.

Finally he turned to his mother. "Great dinner, Ma. Thanks." He threw his napkin on the table and got the hell out of there.

He figured he'd learned his lesson from that experience. Flynt generally managed to eat with the family two or three times a week, but not anymore. He was going into avoidance mode. No family dinners or get-togethers for a while. He'd give them all—himself included—a chance to get past the fact that Josie was gone.

Saturday night he had dinner at the club. There were rooms upstairs for the members and for guests—the club also operated as a resort of sorts—so Flynt spent the night there. He was waiting in the clubhouse the next morning, ready to get on the links with Tyler, Spence and Luke.

Again, Luke didn't show. But Michael did.

Flynt played badly. He had a hell of a time keeping his mind on the game.

Later he ate in the Grill with the men. Spence told them that he'd hired Ben Ashton. The P.I. would have a first report for them in a few weeks.

After the meal Flynt returned to the ranch—though he was under no illusions that anyone there would be glad to see him. Except for Lena. She smiled and laughed and waved her fat little hands at him, totally unaware that no one else in the house wanted a damn thing to do with him.

But hell. His mother and father and sisters and brother had been mad at him before. It hadn't killed him.

Losing Josie, though, that just might. In the day, he couldn't stop thinking of her.

And at night, it only got worse.

He was in his study around four, balancing a few accounts, when Matt buzzed him on the house line.

"I need to talk to you," his brother said.

"Okay. Talk."

Complaints followed. A string of them. Problems in the breeding program, fences down, miles of them. Hands that had gone off and got drunk and not come back to work.

It was all just routine stuff.

But for some reason, Matt had decided it was all Flynt's fault.

"Damn it, what's eating you?" Flynt finally barked into the phone.

Matt said something ugly and hung up on him.

Very carefully Flynt put the phone back in its cradle. He wanted to break something. He wanted a drink.

Most of all, he wanted Josie.

Unfortunately it was a none-of-the-above situation. He decided he had to get out of there. He returned to the club, ate in the Grill and again spent the night in one of the big suites upstairs.

Monday morning he decided he was through living at the club just because his brother was a fight waiting to happen. Flynt went home. He was hard at work in his study when his mother tapped on the door.

She came in and stood opposite his desk and looked at him with her sweetest, most conciliatory expression. "Flynt, we're all upset to lose Josie."

As if he wasn't. "Got that. Loud and clear."

"We all could see how much you two loved each other and it simply makes no sense to us that you couldn't work out your differences." She paused, waiting, he knew, for him to say something.

No way.

Eventually she heaved a big sigh and went on. "But honestly, we don't want to let this drive a wedge between us. Let's all try to get along, can't we?"

"Ma, I am doing my best and that's a damn fact."

"Join the family for dinner tonight, won't you?"

He should have said no. But he never could refuse his mother when she gave him that pleading look she was giving him right then. "I'll be there."

She thanked him and left.

That night both Cara and Fiona ate elsewhere. There were just the four of them: Ford, Grace, Matt and Flynt.

His parents put some real effort into making the whole thing bearable. They talked of the weather, of how well that remodeling project in Corpus was going.

Matt scowled and glowered and muttered one-syllable answers to any questions directed his way. Flynt tried not to get into it with him. He honestly did.

Somehow they made it through the soup and the salad. The maid had just set their T-bones in front of them when Matt looked over and asked, "So, Mr. President, you gonna hang out at the club for the rest of your life, wheeling and dealing and practicing your sand wedge—or you think maybe I could get a little damn help around here now and then?"

It was enough. Way more than enough.

Flynt threw down his napkin and stood. "You want a piece of me, Matt?" Grace gasped. Flynt ignored her. "Is that what we're dealing with here?"

Matt shoved back his chair.

Ford said, "Now, boys…"

Flynt hardly heard him. He'd gone past the point where a "Now, boys" could stop him. His blood seemed to pound, hot and insistent, through his veins. "Come on. You want it, you got it."

"Not in the house!" Grace cried. But the two of them had already stepped free of the table.

Matt came at him, fast. Flynt crouched down to meet him, butting him in the midsection with his head. Matt let out a hard grunt and grabbed on.

They went down to the rug, rolling, trading

punches, bumping into the furniture, sending breakable things like lamps and vases crashing to the floor.

Matt got the upper hand. He rolled on top and sat up and Flynt took one on the jaw and another one hard on the cheekbone.

Looming above him, Matt glared down. "You damn, stupid fool. You got it all and you toss it over. The only thing standin' between you and what you love is *you*. I'd give my right arm to be in your boots, you know that? And if I was, you can be damn sure I wouldn't throw it all away. If I was you, I wouldn't—"

Flynt didn't want to hear it—mostly because it rang all too true. He gave a heave with his midsection. It worked—at least to a degree. Matt flew forward on top of him and then they were rolling again.

Ford was shouting. Grace, too.

"Stop, now!"

"You boys, you stop right now!"

Flynt gained the top position. He reared up on his brother and he gave him two hard jabs, a left and a right.

Matt grunted twice. He had blood on his face and in his hair, not only from the blows Flynt had delivered, but from the bits of broken china and glass they were rolling in. Flynt knew he looked about the same.

Not that he cared.

He cared for nothing. Not anymore. There was

himself. There was his adversary. There was the next blow.

He brought back his fist to deliver that blow.

Two sets of strong arms stopped him.

Someone must have run out and called in a few of the ranch hands.

"Easy, now. Easy does it," one of the hands muttered.

It took three of them to pull him off Matt and another two to hold Matt back from jumping him again.

Ford stepped between them. "All right, boys. You've had your fun. It's over. Calm down."

Matt and Flynt agreed to pay for what they'd broken. Then they made up, more or less.

Matt admitted he was out of line. "I'm kind of on edge lately, you know?"

Flynt accepted his brother's apology. The thrill of the fight was behind them. Now came that dust-and-ashes feeling, that time when a man wondered what the hell it had even been about.

Grace wanted to herd the two of them to the big bathroom off the kitchen and patch them up the way she used to do when they were kids.

Flynt shook his head. "Thanks anyway, Ma." He looked around at the mess they had made. "I'm damn sorry about this."

"Now, now," said Grace. "They're only things…"

He made his excuses and he got out of there, climbing the stairs, headed for his own wing. When he got there, he should have gone straight to his bedroom suite, stripped off his clothes and got himself into the shower. But he didn't. He entered his study and he shut the door.

Then he took a key from his desk and went to the cabinet next to the credenza. He kept the scotch in that cabinet, for the occasional meeting when someone wanted a drink.

There was no meeting now. He was alone. With that gray, bleak dust-and-ashes feeling.

Alone and finally admitting that he'd fought this battle long enough. That he was tired all the way to the bone, plain wrung-out with fighting—both his brother and the hell inside his own mind—and he wanted a damn drink.

He deserved a damn drink.

He stuck the key into the lock and gave it a turn. And then the cabinet was open and the Chivas was right there in front of him. He reached for the bottle and grabbed a short glass from a shelf. He poured out three fingers, then splashed in more.

"For good measure," he said aloud to the silent room.

Nobody answered.

What a surprise.

He set the open bottle on the credenza and brought the glass to his mouth. The smell of it filled his nostrils—strong and sweet, with the promise of comfort. Of that slow, drifting feeling, and then, sometime later, a welcome oblivion.

He put the glass to his lips.

And he heard his brother's voice.

You damn, stupid fool. You got it all and you toss it over. The only thing standin' between you and what you love is you....

Flynt blinked, pulled the glass away just enough that he could look into it.

Josie's face.

Oh, yeah. He could see her. Looking at him the same way she'd looked at him a year and a half ago, that morning when she finally doused him with ice water and told him off for hiding from his life—and his guilt—in a bottle.

He blinked again.

Her face was gone.

But still, he stared into the amber depths.

So, he thought, is this what it's come to, then? Now I go back to drinking my life away in order to bear the damn mess I've made of everything?

What had she said, a week ago, when he told her he wanted her out of his life?

That he couldn't go back. He only had now. And if he didn't live now, he might as well be in the grave with his dead wife and lost baby.

Evil, she'd called it. To let himself love her only for duty's sake.

Right then it came to him. The question that turned his whole world around.

What good did it do the dead? What would Monica and the baby get out of it if he wasted the rest of his life as a damn drunk, if he loved no one, gave nothing, brought no new life into the world?

Flynt set the untouched glass gently down.

Maybe, he thought, the only thing a man could do for the ones that were gone was to live the life he had left fully and well.

Seventeen

Flynt Carson went after his woman the next day. He hardly slept the night before. He tossed and turned, fighting the urge to go to her sooner.

But he figured he'd done enough chasing after her in darkness.

It was time he declared himself in the bright light of day.

He had a big doubt inside him, gnawing away like a mean rat—that she wouldn't take him back, wouldn't give him one more chance.

The truth was, he couldn't blame her if she turned him down. He'd put her through hell and she deserved better than the likes of him. If she sent him packing, he'd live through it.

Somehow.

But he wouldn't lose her for lack of trying.

He went to Alva's house first. He waited on her sagging front porch, his heart pounding hard and his palms wet, for someone to answer his knock.

Finally Alva pulled the door back. She looked at him through narrowed eyes. "She's not here."

Flynt rarely wore a hat, except when he worked the

ranch alongside his brother, but he wore a straw Resistol that day. He knew he needed to have his hat in his hands. "Please, Mrs. Lavender." He turned the hat by the brim as he spoke. Every nerve he had was singing, calling Josie's name. "I know I'm not good enough for your daughter, but I love her. And you could say I have seen the light."

"What happened to your face, Flynt Carson?"

Yeah, all right. He was a mess. Cuts on his neck and his jaw from rolling in broken glass, a black eye and a goose egg at the high point of his right cheek. "I ran into a door."

Alva smiled then. "Maybe a couple of doors."

"That's right, ma'am. Maybe even three or four. I've got to pay more attention to where I'm going, and that is a fact."

Alva peered at him closely, as if making sure of something. And then she said, "Try the Mission Creek Café."

When Flynt walked into the Mission Creek Café, Josie was serving toast and tea to Mavis, Anna and TildyLee, three sweet little ladies who came in every Tuesday at ten.

They liked having Josie wait on them because she always took time with them. And she never ran out of patience when they got their orders confused, which, somehow, they always did.

"No, now, Anna, that English muffin, I believe, is mine. You had a blueberry muffin, didn't you?"

"TildyLee, I did not. That English muffin is mine. You had wheat toast. And the sourdough goes to Mavis."

Mavis let out a little chirp of outrage. "No, it does not. I didn't have sourdough. I don't even *like* sourdough."

"Well, then, why did you order it?"

"I *didn't* order it."

"Mavis Letha Enderberry, you know that you did."

Josie stood by the table, holding all three orders, letting the ladies get the arguing out of their systems. Eventually she'd serve whatever they still wanted—and go back for replacements of whatever wouldn't do. She had a feeling the sourdough was out of there. And maybe even the wheat toast. The only sure thing right then was that both TildyLee and Anna wanted the muffin.

She was vaguely aware that the door to the street opened. She heard the bell warning them a new customer had entered.

And then she heard nothing.

A kind of stillness.

It was as if everyone in the café—well, except for the three ladies arguing over their muffins and toast—had turned to stare at whoever had just come in.

Ellie Switzer said, "Oh, my!"

And Margie Dodd whistled. "Well, what have we here?"

Josie turned to see what was so interesting—and almost dropped the plates she had in her hands.

"Careful, dear," cautioned TildyLee.

"Whoopsy," chirped Mavis with a girlish giggle.

Flynt!

Her foolish heart seemed to shout his name.

He looked just awful. All cut up and bruised. He'd been in a fight somewhere, that much was certain. He was headed right for her and she didn't know what to do.

Run to his arms? Run away as fast as her feet would carry her? Stand her ground and find out just what he was doing here?

She ended up standing her ground, but more out of shock than any kind of real choice.

"Josie," he said when he reached her and stood looking down at her. He said it as if the whole world was held in her name.

She gulped. "What?" She made herself glare at him. "What do you want, Flynt Carson?"

"You," he said softly. He had a hat—he never wore a hat. But today, he had a hat. And it was in his hands.

She gulped again.

Margie appeared at her elbow. "Better let me have those plates." Margie took the two orders of toast and the muffin and she turned and set them on the edge of the table where the three ladies—all very quiet now—sat. "Work it out," she said in a tone of cool command.

"Well, all right," said Mavis. "I will eat that sourdough."

Flynt said, "One more chance, Josie. Give me one more chance. You won't regret it. I swear that you won't."

She stared up at him, loving him so much, it was a throbbing ache inside her, knowing she was a goner, wondering why it was her destiny to be such a total fool for this man.

Then he got down on one knee. He caught her hand. And he kissed it.

Even Margie sighed when he did that.

"I love you, Josie Lavender. You are the woman for me. I have been blind and I have been dead wrong. And I've hurt you, bad. I know I have. I don't deserve the love of a woman like you. But damn it, just try me again. Marry me. Marry me now. Right away. As soon as we can get ourselves a license. Let's make the life we're meant to make, you and me side by side."

"Oh," she said, twin tears forming, escaping, sliding down her cheeks. "Oh, why am I such a sucker for you, Flynt Carson?"

He put his hat against his chest. "Was that a yes?"

She bit her lip to stop the flood of tears that threatened to come pouring out. And she nodded.

He stood and swept her up in his big arms and carried her out of there.

No one said a word until the door swung shut behind them.

Then Ellie burst into tears.

Gus turned to her and shouted, "Get to work! I don't pay you for blubberin'."

Margie Dodd asked the three ladies, "Is everybody happy?"

TildyLee replied with a sigh of pure delight, "Oh, yes. We are just fine. And isn't love grand?"

Epilogue

Flynt had meant what he said. He wanted them married immediately. But Grace insisted that they must have a proper wedding and a huge reception.

Both the groom and his mother got what they were after. Flynt pulled a few strings and lined up the club's ballroom for that Saturday afternoon. Grace, Ford, Cara and Fiona started making calls. Josie was hustled right over to Mission Creek Creations to get herself a wedding dress. Flowers were ordered, a band hired, the menu planned, all in record time. Grace was in her element. She even made time to help Alva pick out a lovely sky-blue ensemble to wear as mother of the bride. And Josie made sure her friends at the café and up in Hurst were invited.

Saturday at one in the afternoon, Josie and Flynt said their vows at First Church, with Reverend Williams presiding. The ceremony itself was small—just the immediate family.

But the party after, in the vast upstairs ballroom at the Lone Star Country Club, was an event to remember. It seemed to Josie that everyone in the county showed up.

To kick off the festivities, Josie stepped out on the dance floor with Flynt for the first dance. It was just the two of them, gliding across the floor under the glittering crystal chandeliers.

Flynt bent close and whispered, "What are you thinking, Mrs. Carson?"

She whispered back, "That maybe I'm not so naive, after all."

Flynt laughed and kissed her and all the guests applauded and Josie blushed. For a moment there, she'd actually forgotten that she and Flynt weren't alone.

They stayed on that floor until the band took its first break. Then they sat for a while with Ford and Grace and Alva. Eventually Josie excused herself for a visit to the special powder room reserved just for the bride.

It was a lovely little space, with a wide, well-lighted mirror and a dressing table. Josie used the stall and was washing her hands in the marble sink when the door opened.

She gasped. "Rose." She dried her hands quickly and rushed to her secret friend. The two women embraced.

Rose whispered, "I heard you and Flynt were getting married. Wainwrights aren't welcome, of course, but I couldn't resist sneaking in to wish you… everything. Love and happiness. Lots of laughter. Joy. All the wonderful things you so richly deserve."

"Oh, I'm so glad that you did." Josie took her friend by the shoulders and held her away enough that their eyes could meet. She didn't like what she saw. "Rose, are you all right?"

"Fine, really. Just a little tired." She looked away, then back. "I broke it off with Matt."

Josie just ached for her. "Don't give up. I know it will work out. Hey, it worked out for me, didn't it?"

Rose forced a smile. "One more hug. A big one, for luck."

They embraced once more, and then Rose slipped out.

Josie sank to the cushioned chair at the dressing table, shaking her head and cursing that stupid, decades-old feud. Then she put on fresh lipstick and went back out to join her bridegroom.

Three hours later, she stood at the top of the wide staircase that led down to the clubhouse lobby, her groom at her side, her bouquet of lilies and roses in her hand. Below on the lobby floor, all the single women looked up at her, their dreams in their eyes.

Josie gazed down over the sea of hopeful faces and spotted a certain one on the edge of the crowd. She lifted a brow in question and got a quick nod in response.

Raising her bouquet, she sent it soaring out. Down below, all the single ladies held up eager hands to catch it. But it sailed right past them and dropped into the waiting arms of the slim, black-haired woman at the edge of the crowd.

"My God," someone cried. "Did you see that? That was Rose Wainwright."

The name spread through the crowd. "Rose Wainwright."

"Rose Wainwright. Did you see her?"

"Rose Wainwright has caught the Carson bride's bouquet."

"Over there. She was over there."

But the slender, dark-haired woman had already slipped away.

Flynt whispered into Josie's ear, "Tell me that didn't happen."

"Well, I can't tell you that." She turned and put her hands on his broad chest. "Because it did."

He frowned down at her. "Was that Rose Wainwright?"

"Maybe."

"Is that all you're going to say?"

"'Fraid so, for right now." She twined her arms around his neck.

"What?" he muttered darkly.

"I'm kind of hoping you'll kiss me."

Slowly he smiled. "Josie Carson, that's a request I can't refuse."

And then, oh so tenderly, he lowered his mouth to hers.

* * * * *

*Don't miss the next story from
Silhouette's*
LONE STAR COUNTRY CLUB:

TEXAS ROSE
by Marie Ferrarella
Available July 2002
(ISBN:0-373-61353-9)

*Turn the page for an excerpt from this
exciting romance...!*

One

"Whose is it, girl?"

Archy Wainwright's question exploded like thunder, swallowing up the deathlike silence that had come a moment before. Stunned silence had been the initial reaction to Rose's quietly spoken announcement, delivered at the dining-room table where her father, sister and brother had gathered for dinner.

If she'd had her choice, Rose Wainwright would have opted to spare her family the news altogether. Hearing that his unmarried, thirty-year-old librarian daughter was pregnant wasn't exactly something a father wanted to hear—least of all the stern, volatile Archy Wainwright, respected land baron and patriarch of one of the two oldest families in Mission Creek, Texas.

But it wasn't as if she could keep it a secret indefinitely. Even now, only six weeks along, Rose was certain she would begin showing at any moment. Despite the fact that her clothes fit just the way they always had, she felt huge.

Maybe it was the overwhelming weight of her secret that made her feel this way.

Or maybe it was because her world had been stood on its ear ever since she'd stood in the bathroom within her wing of the sprawling ranch house, holding her breath, waiting for a small stick to decide her fate.

No, Rose amended, that wasn't really true. Her world had been upended ever since she'd first succumbed to Matt's charms and fallen in love with him. Ever since she'd first laid eyes on him. He'd leaned over the library counter and asked, with that devil of a twinkle in his beautiful blue eyes, if he could take out anything he found within the library. When she'd answered a tentative "yes," he'd put his hand on hers and said that what he really wanted to take out was the librarian.

Rose remembered blushing to the roots of her jet-black hair. Even so, she'd taken exception to Matt's unabashed flirtation. She'd been schooled to be cautious because he was, after all, who he was. A Carson. The enemy. Forbidden fruit.

She, a Wainwright, was pregnant by a Carson.

And nobody was ever going to find out that part.

Telling her father would unleash a torrent of trouble that could only be equaled to the tumultuous origins of the feud that had separated the two once-friendly families and placed them on opposing ends of everything for the last seventy-five years.

Because it was unthinkable for a Carson and a

Wainwright to actually entertain the idea of marriage, she deliberately hadn't told Matt that she was carrying his baby. She was afraid he'd do something stupid, like marry her because of the baby and estrange himself from his family. It was a guilt she felt unequal to bearing.

Worse still, she couldn't bear the thought that he might turn his back on her and tell her she was on her own. That getting pregnant was her fault, despite the precautions she'd taken.

Though the thought of bearing Matt's child had drawn her closer to him emotionally, Rose had gone out of her way to instigate an argument that had led to the end of their clandestine affair.

The day she'd broken it off was painful. She'd lied for the very first time in her life and told Matt that she was no longer excited by being with him. That she was bored of it all and of him.

The words had tasted bitter in her mouth. More bitter still had been the look she'd seen in his eyes. His beautiful blue eyes had pain in them. Pain she had put there.

Now her father's eyes pinned her to her chair, willing his daughter to answer.

"Well?" he demanded again. "Who's the tomcat who's been sniffing around your skirts, girl? What's the name of the man whose hide I'm going to nail to the barn door?" His eyes became small slits beneath his bushy eyebrows. "Out with it, Rosie."

She lifted her chin. "No."

"No?" Archy thundered in disbelief. Rose had never been this blatantly defiant before, never challenged his authority.

"Why won't you tell me who the father is, girl?" Archy barked.

Rose felt like crying. Like screaming. Ever since this baby had been formed, her emotions felt as if they were on a constant roller-coaster ride.

"Because you'd kill him and then Justin would have to arrest you," Susan spoke up, coming to her older sister's defense.

Rose wished her father would drop this already. "It's my business who the father is."

"And what happens within this family is mine." He paused, gathering himself. "I'm not going to have people flapping their jaws about you like you were common trash. You're going to live with my sister until this blows over."

"But Aunt Beth is in New York," Rose protested.

Archy loomed over his daughter, in no mood to put up with any more opposition.

"So?" he demanded.

It was on the tip of her tongue to say that she didn't want to go to New York, but then Rose thought better of it. Maybe distance from everything and everyone was the best way to go right now. She certainly couldn't go on living here with her father's accusatory looks. More important, she couldn't remain in Mission Creek, running the risk of bumping into Matt.

If he saw her pregnant, there'd be no question in his mind that it was his. If he did do the so-called "honorable" thing and asked her to marry him, she might not have the strength to say no. And then there'd be a showdown between the two men she loved most: her father and Matt. That was something she definitely didn't want to have on her conscience.

"So I'll pack," Rose finally said. With that, she turned on her heel, leaving the members of her family looking at one another in mute surprise and confusion.

"In a real short amount of time, Rosie's gotten to be a very contrary girl," Archy muttered more to himself than to the others at the table. "Even when she's doing what you think you want her to." He shook his head. "Just like her mother."